DREAM'S LIFE 2

AMILIA'S CHAOS

ASSA RAYMOND BAKER

Good2Go Publishing

Dream's Life 2
Written by Assa Raymond Baker
Cover Design: Davida Baldwin
Typesetter: Mychea
ISBN: 9781947340213
Copyright © 2018 Good2Go Publishing
Published 2018 by Good2Go Publishing
7311 W. Glass Lane • Laveen, AZ 85339
www.good2gopublishing.com
https://twitter.com/good2gobooks
G2G@good2gopublishing.com
www.facebook.com/good2gopublishing
www.instagram.com/good2gopublishing

ACKNOWLEDGMENTS

All praise be to God, Lord of my life.

As always, I thank G2G. I thank Davida for the work on the cover design that I wouldn't have ever thought of. I thank Mychea for powering through my dyslexic spells. I thank Ray for all of this. I thank my five-star queens for their unconditional love and keeping me focused behind these walls.

I thank all my brothas and gangstas for looking past their flags to come together and try to keep these youngstas from coming back behind these walls once they're released.

I thank all of you readers! I wish I could break down and give y'all my chronicles uncut, but I can't, and it's more fun this way. I don't write for the money. I don't write for the fame. I don't even write for y'all. I write for myself in hopes that it's entertaining to y'all. I write because it's my escape from these cell walls. I thank all of you out there screaming "Free Assa Ray" and all of y'all who take the time to correspond with me via snail mail.

Okay, well I gotta get back to work. Assa out!

PROLOGUE

Amilia sat alone inside the immaculate Gomez mansion on the two-year anniversary of the tragic week that ripped her family apart. It was the week when her husband, Cheez, was murdered and her daughter accidentally overdosed a few days later. Now Amilia sat on the bed in her daughter's old bedroom that she refused to allow anyone to enter. She was on her second bottle of red wine while looking over the family photo album. It was an accident that took her child from her, but Amilia still blamed herself for not disposing of Cheez's pain meds after his murder.

"I'm sooo sorry, baby! I've been sitting here, just sitting here feeling like crap for being a bad mother. No! I'm a good mother! It's not all my fault! That whore, Dream, is the bitch to blame! It's all because of her that you and your father aren't here with me now," she cried as she spoke to the smiling faces in the photo on the last day they were all together as a family.

"That bitch needs to pay for what she caused. She needs to feel my pain and more, and I'm going to see to it that she does. Why should she have her daughter and happiness, when all I have is pain and more pain!" she yelled, and then took a sloppy drink from the bottle, spilling wine down her shirt in her drunken state of anger.

"Oops! Mommy made a mess!" she sighed as she tried to get to her feet.

DREAM'S LIFE 2

AMILIA'S CHAOS

CHAPTER 1

Enough Is Enough!

Secret had moved into one of the guest rooms the day after he had killed Cheez, so he could be there to console Amilia and the kids in their time of mourning. They were careful not to let the kids know about their affair so soon after their father's death. Tonight, when Secret made it home, he found the place cool and quiet, and he knew that his girl was having another one of her bad days. He removed his gun and phones before going to search for her. This time he found Amilia passed out on the floor of the kids' bathroom with a knocked over bottle of wine not far from her.

This was becoming a monthly routine for him to find her somewhere drunk and passed out whenever he took her son for the weekend or to give her a break. Amilia would use the time to drink herself to sleep, after punishing herself in the gym for hours on and off throughout the day. Secret knew she was hurting, and he wished she would just tell him what she needed from him to make the pain stop. He also knew that she could never find out that he was the one who started the ball rolling that had caused her so much pain and heartbreak.

Secret wasn't thinking about Amilia's children when he carried out her father's orders and murdered Cheez. He was only thinking of the reward of getting the woman he loved and becoming the new face of the Gomez syndicate in the States. He now almost had all of what he wanted. The only thing missing was his queen.

They hadn't had sex for ten months straight now. The last time they really made love was on the night they woke up and found Amilia's daughter lying on the floor with an empty bottle of powerful pain pills lying on the bed.

Secret gently picked up Amilia and undressed her before placing her in the shower and turning on the cold water. He wanted to get her sobered up enough to feed her and then put her to bed.

"Awwwwh!" she snapped awake from the sudden cold water on her bare skin.

"You were passed out on the floor. You can't keep drinking like this, Amilia. You can't keep going on like this, for real!" he told her, standing outside of the frosted glass shower door.

"I'm sorry! I'm sorry, Secret! Baby, please don't leave me! You're all I have, now that my mother has taken my son from me!"

"No! Never, ma! I'm not going nowhere, and it's up to you to get your son back. Look at yourself, Amilia. Do you want him to see you broken like this?"

Secret knew her son was with the grandparents, but he didn't know that they weren't planning on giving him back to her this time.

"No!" Amilia answered, sounding almost child-like while she was still under the spray of water.

"You don't need to be apologizing to me. Just please tell me what you need so I can help. I'll do anything to make your pain stop. Just talk to me!" he said as he stepped out of his shoes and socks and then walked into the shower with her while still in his clothes. "I miss you. I need you to come back to us. I love you! You know it! And you know all you have to do is ask for my help and mean it when you do, and I'm there!" he promised her as he pulled her up off the floor and into his strong arms.

"Help me!" Amilia pulled away from him so she

could look him in the eyes. "Help me! Make me feel again. Let me feel you!" she begged, with tears coming down just as hard as the spray of water they were standing beneath.

"I got you. Just not like this!" he said sincerely, pulling her head to his chest and kissing the top of it. "Amilia, finish your shower and meet me in the kitchen. I know you haven't eaten, so we can talk more while we eat."

Secret kissed her on the forehead and allowed her to lean into him. He then kissed her on the lips before he stepped out of the shower soaking wet.

"Secret, wait!" she called out louder than she had intended. "All I want you to do is kill that whore, Dream! I'm like this because of her!"

~ ~ ~

Secret cooked his famous bacon and jalapeño grilled cheese sandwiches while he was in the kitchen. He also put on a fresh pot of strong coffee.

While preparing the light hangover meal, Amilia's request kept replaying in his mind. Somehow, he always knew that the day would come when he would be asked to address the issue in Milwaukee with Dream and her friends. Secret didn't mind the request. He was actually relieved that she hadn't asked him to do anything stupid like take her son back from her parents or, worse, kill her father. Amilia once told him she believed her father was behind the ordered hit on her husband. She said her father took the fact that Cheez put her in a position where she could have been killed as a slap in the face.

"Mmmmmmm! I can't lie. That smells good! I love the smell of bacon and fried onions," Amilia announced as she walked into the kitchen.

She headed straight for the coffee and poured herself a cup, and then took a seat at the counter.

"Papi, I made up my mind. Tonight was the last time you'll ever see me a mess like that again!"

"What did you hit your head on?" he asked.

He noticed a small bruise on her temple as he placed the two sandwiches on a plate next to her.

"I'm not sure!" she replied as she lightly ran her fingers over the blemish on her face. "Papi, I do owe you apologies. For so long we wished that we could be together; and now that we can be, I'm not here the way you need me to be."

Amilia got up, walked over to him, and wrapped her arms around him from behind and hugged him.

"Watch it! You almost touched the stove!" he warned her.

"Let me make it up to you!" she said as she slid her small hand into the top of his sweatpants.

Amilia got seriously turned on by the instant response her touch received as she stroked his semi-hard length.

"Ohhhh, so you do miss me!"

"Why wouldn't I?" he questioned as he spun around to face her, still missing the feel of her coffee-warmed hands on him. "Can a bitch out there take your place in my heart? Not now! Not ever!"

He kissed her longer than he intended to because of the lust building inside of him moment by moment.

"Eat, so you don't get sick, and if you're still up to it afterward, we can continue this."

"Okay, let's eat out on the patio."

Amilia didn't wait for an answer. She simply gathered up the cup and plate and headed outside.

Once out on the patio, Secret admitted that he had been keeping loose tabs on them in Milwaukee for her father. He showed her pictures of Rahji on the playground at the school she attended. It was one of the properties he believed they owned that was under reconstruction and one of the nightclubs they went to on a regular basis.

"I know the house! I have the address from when I was with—!"

"With Cheez? It's okay. You can say his name. You can say whatever you need to, to get this out of your system. I'm here for you, always. I promise!" He held her hand assuredly in his. "Amilia, are you sure you want me to do this? Because all I gotta do is send a text and they're done!"

Amilia said nothing. She just stood up and removed the oversized nightshirt she put on after her shower, which revealed her sexy, curvy nude body. She had given the house staff the rest of the week off after her mother had taken her child, so she felt okay with exposing herself to her man outside and under the fading night sky. But what Amilia did not know was that her father had ordered his men to watch over the house at all times, and no one overrules the old man's orders.

Webb was making a quick outer perimeter walk when he observed Amilia disrobe. He knew he should have kept moving, but he could not pull his eyes away from the ruthless crime boss's daughter's naked body. He took a step back so his shadow would not be cast out by the moonlight. He then watched lustfully as Amilia held out her hands to Secret.

"I'll have someone get right on it after I handle you then," Secret told her as he pulled her into his arms while kissing away anything else she might have wanted to say on the subject.

Webb continued to watch as Amilia helped his boss out of his clothes, and wished it was his lips on hers.

Secret helped himself to her warm perky nipples by sucking one between his lips while caressing one of her breasts with his free hand. Amilia pulled him down on top of herself as she lay back in the moist grass of the backyard. She then took hold of his impressive erection and dragged the head of it up and around her clit. She teased Secret as well as Webb when he heard her moan.

"Whoa, ma! I got this. Let me do my job and give you what you need," Secret told her in a low, husky voice.

He removed her hand and then pushed hard and

fast into her warmth, causing her to cry out in pleasure for several loud moments before slowing his pace.

Webb was so aroused by the both of them that he pulled out his hardness and began stroking it as he watched the show they were putting on. He was so turned on that it didn't matter to him that the release he was chasing could cost him his life if he was caught. He sped up his strokes almost matching Secret's rhythm until he shot his powerful release into the nothingness of the morning, wishing it was deep inside Amilia.

CHAPTER 2

Rather Be Caught with Than Without

Rahji was away for the night at a fairy-themed slumber party hosted at Nessa's new childcare center. This was after the attempted kidnapping of Rahji that ended with Nessa's cousin, Sam, killing the man in the building. Trigga and Paper came together and gave her enough money to open up a new location on Appleton Avenue. Knowing the princess was in good hands, Dream and Leslie prepared for a night out with their men.

"What's wrong? Why you looking all funny-faced?" Dream asked as she checked herself over in the large vanity mirror.

She was dressed in a cream, printed Gucci romper with matching heels and a colorful icy Pandora charm bracelet. Her outfit was topped off with a simple silver heart-shaped locket around her neck.

"I'm just nervous, I guess!" Leslie admitted.

Leslie was dressed in a fitted, black Dior mini dress with black Jimmy Choo heels. She was also wearing an icy Pandora charm bracelet.

"About what? Girl, what you done did?"

"Nothing yet, but—!"

Leslie turned around on the makeup stool on which she was seated and showed Dream a thick, gold-cluster diamond engagement ring.

"I'm going to ask Paper to marry me tonight. What do you think?"

"Wow! I mean wow!" Dream exclaimed, taking the ring box from her friend's shaky hand. "I think if that man don't say yes, I'ma slap the black off his ass." They laughed. "Why you didn't tell me sooner? I would've loved to have helped you pick this ring," Dream asked as she handed it back to her.

"I don't know. I kinda thought you would tell me it was too soon and you'd try to talk me out of it."

"Sis, it's been over two years since those two wonderful men were thrown into our lives. Look at us!" Dream said as she stepped aside so Leslie could see herself in the full-length mirror as well. "We might not be living if it wasn't for them."

Dream thought about when she fell for Trigga. She told him it was when she saw how he was with her daughter on the plane, but the truth was, the day he came back for them at that ranch in Georgia was the day she fell in love. Dream remembered saying a silent prayer for Trigga as he ran for the car with Cheez's men chasing and shooting at him. Sometimes at night, she sat up in bed afraid to close her eyes because the image of the red mist of Dice's head exploding was too real for her to get to sleep.

"So, I should ask him?" Leslie inquired, bringing Dream back from her memory.

"Damn you, bitch! Now I'm mad that I'm not popping the question with you!"

"Should I wait for you?"

"No! Let tonight be all about you two. Who knows? Trigga might get inspired and ask me himself."

They heard the men pull up into the driveway followed by a text which rushed them out of the house.

"You sure? Because I can wait!"

"Stop trying to use me to get out of it, Leslie. Don't worry! He won't say no. And this is what I get for acting like a girl and not doing what you are about to do."

"Well, you will get left behind if you keep

waiting on a man to do everything!"

They both laughed and headed out of the house.

~ ~ ~

Paper pulled up and stopped in front of ETO's hyped new nightclub on Milwaukee's well-known Water Street. He and Trigga watched as the big-armed bouncer escorted their women past the long line and into the club. Once they saw they were safely inside, Paper spun his rose-orange Infiniti FX35 in a U-turn across the busy avenue, which briefly halted the flow of traffic, so he could park in the spot that was reserved just for them in front of the club.

"Do you really need to be strapped going in there tonight, bro? I mean, ETO has men everywhere!" Paper asked while gathering the two Glock .40s from the stash box.

"Yep, we do!"

"Bro, I just got a funny feeling about tonight, and I ain't trying to get caught up with this burner on a humbug."

"Paper, I told you that as long as you're still fucking around in these streets, we gonna be strapped. Because your ass out here means my ass out here, so you know I'd rather be caught with than without my bitch!" Trigga explained while placing his weapon on his waist before opening the door to exit the truck. "By the way, man, you and sis been acting weird tonight. Is you sure everything's good with you two?"

As Trigga stepped out, his cell phone fell out of his lap and then a few things happened fast. Three men broke away from the crowded line of partygoers that were waiting to be allowed inside the hot spot. Each of the assailants was armed and openly began firing on the truck as they rushed toward it.

Paper was just about to step out but quickly dove back inside using the door for the little bit of shielding it could offer him. He then returned fire through its now shattered driver's-side window.

Trigga threw himself on the ground, rolling over until he could take cover behind one of the 28-inch rims. He then sent blind wild shots at the three men who were shooting at them. He looked up and saw one of the would-be assassins get hit by a speeding Cadillac Escalade and another hit by one of Paper's shots from the window. Just as the second man went down, Trigga spotted a dark gray Dodge Durango come to a hard, screaming stop at the corner. Its driver then started sending rapid shots from a small fully automatic gun. He sprayed both the Cadillac and the Infiniti up to provide cover fire for the two men that were about to make it on their own to him. Once he had them inside, the Durango sped away into the night.

"Trig! Trig, you good, bro?" Paper called out as he slammed a fresh clip into the butt of his gun.

"Yeah! Fuck! I think I broke my hand, but I'm good!" he answered as he quickly climbed to his feet.

"Hey, y'all, this muthafucker's still alive!" Misty informed them from the Escalade.

Misty had walked out of the exit of the club to get ETO's second cell phone just as the shooting started. She looked over and spotted three men rushing up and firing on her friends, and she quickly did what she could to help.

"Misty, we gotta get outta here. Leslie and Dream are already inside. Let 'em know we okay, and make sure they get home!" Paper told her as he found his keys and started the truck so he and Trigga could put some distance between them and the sound of the approaching police cars.

Once Trigga was inside, Paper stormed the truck in the opposite direction of the squads. He prayed that he wasn't driving right into them.

"Bro, do you know what that shit was about?"

"Hell no! I was just gonna ask you the same thing. I couldn't get a good look at them niggas, and the one that Misty hit in the face was too bloody to see."

"I didn't see none of 'em either, and the Durango looked like a rental to me," Trigga said, gritting his teeth from the pain on his now badly swollen hand.

"That looks bad, bro. Let's get outta this piece of shit so I can get you to the hospital. Hey, do you got your phone?"

"Yeah, I got it!"

He picked it up with his good hand from between his legs. He looked at the screen and saw that he had already received a ton of missed calls and texts from Dream and others who knew him.

"Let me tell them to meet us at the ER so they don't worry so much."

"Tell sis to let Les know that I'm good, and that my cell phone is someplace in the back of the truck. It slid back there when we took off!" Paper said as he

16

zigzagged through the side streets to avoid the police.

Paper took them to Trigga's eastside home because it was the closest to them. He stashed the bullet-riddled truck there behind the house and then hopped in Dream's Volvo wagon and headed to St. Mary's Hospital.

CHAPTER 3

Strike One

In the shadows, Secret sat on a black and deep-purple motorcycle watching the three morons' failed hit. But he had to admire how the two men didn't hesitate or panic when the bullets started flying. Secret then turned his attention to the man who his men had left behind, and decided to shut him up before he could think of talking to the police.

The Milwaukee Police Department had officers surrounding the entire crime scene. They were talking to as many witnesses as they could to gather an idea of what had gone down outside of the club that triggered the shooting. Most of the partygoers' injuries occurred when they ran and fell down when the gunplay began. But two of them were hit by stray bullets. One had non-life-threatening injuries; however, one did die from a gunshot to the back of the head as she ran for cover.

Secret spotted the perfect opportunity to make his move. He eased the bike closer to the ambulance as a few paramedics were pushing the half-conscious hit man on a gurney. When they were just a few feet away, Secret drew his gun and did his best to empty the clip into the body of his target without hitting any of the paramedics.

When his gun clicked empty, Secret jetted off on the powerful Ducati crotch rocket before the police could scramble together to make a real effort to give chase. All the EMTs and the police could do was change their witness, suspect, and hit man's condition from critical to deceased.

CHAPTER 4

Bad Breaking News

Amilia sat alone in one of the plush chairs in Secret's penthouse suite and watched channel 58 news. Secret had already called her with the bad news and told her that he would be there as soon as he had a talk with his men. After the call, Amilia got up and paced angrily around the room until breaking news was announced on the television.

"I understand that you caught the shooting all on video?" the reporter asked as she swung the mic in front of the witness to answer.

"Yes, I got most of it!"

"Can you tell me what the video will show us about what happened here tonight?"

"Man, it's gonna show everything! I got the three guys who started it all by shooting at some other guys parked in a truck. I even got when that girl accidentally hit one of them."

With that said, the witness got really animated with the description.

"She smacked him hard with her truck like bam!

And then a guy in another truck got to busting at her and the others. I didn't get the people from the other truck that picked up the two shooters that started it, but it has everything else."

"There you have it. An eyewitness of the gun battle that rocked our city's downtown streets, leaving at least two dead and many others wounded," the reporter announced as the newscast showed a shot of the aftermath.

Amilia screamed in anger slamming the TV remote control to the floor, sending its batteries and bits of broken plastic sliding across the room. She then grabbed the keys to her rental car and rushed out the door. She wanted to witness just how Secret was going to handle the fools that messed everything up.

A short time later, she pulled up and parked at the address that Secret had texted to her to program into her GPS. She was escorted inside by a young thug who introduced himself as Uriah. Once they were inside, the first thing she saw was a dirty cage that housed two monster-looking pit bulls. She then noticed how clean the rest of the place was to be a dope spot.

"I don't need to know how shit went down,

because I was there watching you fools the whole time. I have it on my phone because I gotta show this shit to a member of the Gomez family who's not gonna be happy when I do. I just wanna fucking know how all this went down and what your fucking plan was!" Secret asked Jorge, who was the one he put in charge and also the driver of the Durango.

"My plan was to catch them off guard, put in the work, and get outta there, but we kinda underestimated them niggas. It was like they were ready for us or something."

"Yeah, Secret. We ended up being the ones caught off guard," José spoke up.

He was the only one of the trio that didn't get a scratch on him.

"You fucking failed. That's it! That's all!" Secret snapped, knowing that Amilia would want to see blood behind this. "You were supposed to hit everyone in the truck. Not let anyone make it out!"

"So, what do we do here in Milwaukee with failures?" Amilia asked as she walked up and stood next to Secret.

"Ma, it's all the same. Failure is unacceptable in any hood, and it's punishable by blood!" he answered as he pulled out his gun.

"No, papi! You've gotten your hands dirty enough tonight," she said as she touched his hand for him to lower his gun. "Uriah!"

"What up, bossy?" The eager youngster sprang to her side.

"Bossy. I like that name." Amilia smiled. "Do you think you can do better at making me happy than these two dumbasses?"

"Bitch, you need to stay in your place. Secret, is this how it's going to be now? You got a bitch giving you orders now?" Jorge asked angrily, not knowing who he was talking to.

Secret punched him in the mouth, knocking him off of his feet.

"This bitch is a Gomez! And I don't believe Mr. Gomez would like anyone talking to his daughter like that!"

"Oh no, he wouldn't!" Amilia said, still smiling as she took the gun from Secret's hand and passed it over to Uriah. "Uriah, I asked you a question before this waste opened his mouth. Show your bossy that you know what makes her happy!"

"Say no mo'!"

Uriah promptly shot both Jorge and José twice, killing them instantly.

"Boots, you and Wicked clean this up, and give Secret a clean gun," Uriah ordered as he commenced to dismantling the gun right there on the spot so his bosses could see that he had their backs.

"I'm good now that this shit is all on you. But just to be on the safe side, Uriah, you need to take care of what's his name. The one who got shot."

"Andre!"

"Whatever! Take care of him, because that fool can't shoot for shit or he really wasn't trying to hit them niggas," Secret told him as he delivered the unknown gun.

"I'll hit you when it's done. Is there something else y'all need me to do?"

"Yeah, get them dogs a bigger cage, and let them out of there and clean them up. Look at them. They can barely move around in there," Amilia said as she walked over and pressed her hand to the cage so the two monsters could get her scent.

After Uriah agreed, Amilia took Secret by the hand and led him back out the way they entered. They then raced back to their suite. She took her rented Pontiac G6 while Secret hopped onto his powerful bike.

~ ~ ~

"Uriah, come to bed, or did you just come over here to do whatever it is you're in there stressing over?" Eve whined from the bedroom's doorway, dressed only in a short lacey muumuu to give him easy access to her pleasure zone.

"In a second! I'm trying to see something. I told you that I got Jorge's spot today, and I have to show 'em that I can handle it," he explained, never looking away from the computer monitor.

Uriah knew he needed to know exactly who he was up against, so he decided to go through all of the different social media postings of the nightclub shooting.

"Bae, they gave it to you because you do everything anyway, and they finally saw it. So I doubt that they'd just take it back like that."

"No they didn't! Bossy didn't even know me. She just liked my swag or something. You know a young gangsta be affecting you bitches in different ways," he told her, just as he clicked on something that he thought could help him. "Eve, I know this truck and this bitch!'" he excitedly said to her.

"So do that mean you can stop now and come handle the effect you having on this bitch right here?" Eve asked, now standing behind him half being nosey while rubbing on his shoulders.

Eve enjoyed the feel of his hard body under her fingers. Uriah stood only five foot seven and weighed about 155 pounds, but he was solid and very toned. Eve loved his Latino confidence and gangster ways.

"Pass me my cell off the couch, and then I'm all yours!"

Uriah sent a text to Secret informing him that he may have a lead on someone that he believed was connected to the group they wanted to hit.

He then spun around in the leather computer chair and pulled his girlfriend into his lap. She kissed and humped him like it was her last time to be with him. He broke their kiss and reached up and ripped off her muumuu to give himself better access to her perky breasts. Eve didn't mind his roughness; in fact, it turned her on even more. She reached down between the two of them and freed his hardness from his jeans and boxers, and then straddled it. She took him all the way inside of her hungry wetness. They kissed more wildly with his full length buried deep yet unmoving inside her. When Uriah couldn't take just sitting there while she came in little squirts on him, he took hold of her throat and waist and lifted her up with him. He then stood up out of the chair and placed her firmly on the soft carpeted floor.

"Mmmm, fuck me! I need it hard!" she encouraged him while locking her long legs behind his head, so he could give her all of what she was begging for. And he did just that.

CHAPTER 5

No Better Time

It had been more than a year since Paper and Leslie
had slept under the same roof as Dream and Trigga.
Leslie couldn't get to sleep after the four of them
made it home from the hospital. She was glad that
Trigga's injury wasn't more serious. His hand wasn't
broken. It was just badly bruised from the way he fell
on it. Leslie was up worrying about what had
happened outside the club, even though Paper swore
to her that they didn't know why they were attacked
and promised that he didn't have any issues with
anyone. She just couldn't make herself believe that
was the last of it.

"Hey, bae, was I snoring again?" Paper asked
when he opened his eyes and found her staring at the
ceiling.

"Baby, you're always snoring. It's just
sometimes louder than others. I'm not up because of
you. It's the memories of how we got together and
all that we've been through together."

"Leslie, if you're still tripping on last night, stop!

They had to have the wrong niggas when they came at us!" Paper said as he propped himself up on the pillows and headboard.

"You know I'm still trippin' about that shit! Y'all could've been killed. But that's not all!" she began as she reached over and dug inside her purse for the black leather ring box. "I don't want to be without you. I need you to know that I'm yours for life through whatever comes our way."

Leslie then handed him the box without opening it.

"What's this?" he asked with a smile as he opened it.

"It's me asking you to marry me!"

"Oh shit! Are you fucking serious right now?" he said as he got up out of the bed, shook his head, and paced back and forth at the foot of the bed. "I can't believe you asked me that!"

"Paper. Baby, I—!"

"I'm not done talking," he cut her off. "Les, you say you know that I love you. Always talking about you know where a nigga's heart is and shit." He then stood in front of her at her side of the bed. "If that's real, hell yeah I'ma marry the fuck outta you!" he answered with a smile bigger than ever.

"You have to say yes. I need to hear you say yes because it's the way I dreamt it would be since I bought the ring," she told him, standing so they were facing each other.

"Well, since this is your show, I want a proper proposal, so get down on your knee!"

He then handed back the box and took a step back to give her space to kneel.

"Okay," Leslie said as she smiled and kissed him and then dragged her nails down his bare chest as she dropped to her knees. "I see you wanna play. I know how to get my yes."

She snatched down his boxers and took his nice morning erection into her mouth.

Leslie used every trick she knew to make him say yes, but it wasn't until she started teasing him by swirling her warm, wet tongue around the head of his length that she got what she wanted and then some as he suddenly filled her mouth with his release.

"Oh shit! Shit! Shit! Whatever you want! Yes!"

~ ~ ~

Trigga and Dream were awakened by Paper's ringtone. She reached over and handed him the phone off the nightstand.

"Nigga, why you calling me this early, bro?" Trigga asked when he answered the phone. "What? That's some real shit! Did she give you a ring and shit?"

Dream could only hear one side of the conversation, but she knew Paper was telling him that Leslie had asked him to marry her. She could hear a shower going in the house, so she guessed that Leslie was the one in it and that was why she hadn't called her to tell her about it yet. Dream didn't really care about her not calling because she wanted to be face-to-face so she could get the story blow-by-blow.

"I'm going to get ready to make breakfast. You better take your meds or that hand's gonna be killing you soon."

"No, let's go out for breakfast so they can tell us this shit in person. You knew she was going to do that, didn't you?"

"Maybe!" she smiled. "Do you want water or juice?"

"Come here!" he said, ending the call with Paper. "Come over here so I can get some of your juice."

"Yeah right! Trigga, you need to put something

on your stomach and take them damn pain meds before you do anything. I'm not trying to be dealing with two babies today."

"You not, because I'm thinking of making one with you right now!" He pulled back the blanket to show her his thickness was standing tall, hard, and ready for her.

"That's not gonna make me change what I said, mister!" She bit her bottom lip with a lustful look in her eyes. "You getting water!" she told him before she marched out of the bedroom and eventually gave in to him.

CHAPTER 6

It Ain't Easy

At noon, ETO, Misty, and one of his young shooters named Boom were all at Trigga's house standing in the backyard watching Paper's Infiniti being loaded onto a flat. ETO was having it towed to the body shop to be repaired.

"You know you don't gotta do this, E!" Paper told him before taking a hit off the blunt.

"Well, homie, that might not be all the way true! The other reason I'm over here is to tell you that Misty found out that the nigga she ran over was a fool named Spade. He ran with them 15s on Walker."

"We had to lay them hoe-ass niggas down last week for jumping two of the lil' homies. I knew they wanted some get-back from all the talking they were doing on Live," Boom explained, just as one of the tires burst on the truck. "Man, they fucked your shit up!"

"Well, shit happens. A nigga will bounce back!" Trigga began as he finished off the blunt. "E, that's good to know, but that shit seems a little more personal to me," he added, pressing the remote start on the Volvo S90.

"Yeah, it looks like that to me too. Me and Leslie been looking at all the posts that people been putting up. They came straight at them, like they knew 'em for sure. Anyway, all y'all just need to be careful!" Dream said in her motherly tone before she hugged Misty and got into the car so Trigga could take her to go pick up her daughter.

"Don't trip! You know how we do. Boom's gonna go holla at 'em and make 'em get their minds right," ETO promised. "And congratulations on the engagement. When y'all set the date, let me host it at the club for y'all. My girl loves planning parties."

"Okay. Yeah, Misty, you gotta get with Les and talk about that. This is her thang. She asked me, but it's still her party."

With that said, they said their goodbyes and went about their business. ETO and the others all climbed back into Boom's blue-and-gold Chevy Equinox sitting on 24-inch matching rims. ETO had Boom follow the tow truck to the body shop so he could personally give them the down payment for both vehicles that were shot up the night before.

On the way, he had Misty pull up the video posts that Dream had mentioned because he hadn't seen them himself. Out of all the things he saw on the video, it was the guy on the motorcycle that concerned him the most. What he did was clean and surely unlike the others.

"Say, homie. Find out who this muthafucka is on this bike when y'all go pay them fools a visit," he ordered Boom.

He then had Misty forward the shot of the guy on the bike to Trigga, asking him if he knew him or had ever seen the bike before.

~ ~ ~

When Amilia finally opened her eyes, Secret had already gone to hook up with Uriah about what he had found. With nothing to do, she spent time on the phone with her mother and son. Hearing her child's voice made her sad, so she decided to find a good gym to go to and work off some of her nervous energy. Amilia hadn't packed any of her workout gear for the trip because she hadn't planned on being in Milwaukee long. But now that she was there, she had to see things through. So Amilia got up, showered, and dressed, and then found the nearest mall to buy a new outfit for the gym, as well as a few other things.

Being out shopping alone was new to her, and it felt freeing to just go and be alone. All Amilia's life she had someone shadowing her every move when she was out and about. That was how she met Cheez. Her father had assigned him to look after her and a few of her girlfriends the very first time Amilia came to the States to visit.

Amilia lost track of the time weaving in and out of different stores and buying things just because they were cute or because the sales clerk was. She was on the third floor of the busy mall when she looked down and unmistakably spotted the person who was at the center of all of her heart's pain. There were Dream, Leslie, and Rahji standing right below her on the first floor clear as day. Amilia's rage took over, and she made a dash toward the nearest set of stairs, leaving her bags behind. She was outnumbered and unarmed, but not defenseless. Amilia had taken up kickboxing as a way to work through her pain, and now she planned to use all her training to kill Dream with her bare hands.

By the time she made it down to the area where

she had seen them standing, they were gone. Amilia rushed back and forth looking through the windows of all the stores on the lower level with no luck. They were just gone. It was almost as if she had imagined it.

"Hey! Hey, excuse me!"

Amilia kept walking and searching the faces in the stores. She was unaware of the young woman who called out to her, until she grabbed her arm.

"What the fuck!" Amilia barked as she snatched away ready to fight.

"I'm sorry to scare you, but I got your stuff. I saw the way you took off running and guessed there had to be something really serious going on down here for you to leave everything like that," she explained, holding up Amilia's purse as well as her shopping bags.

"Oh yes, it was!" Amilia replied as she shook off her anger and forced a smile. "Thank you. My whole world is in this purse. I don't know what I was thinking. Thank you! Here, let me pay you for your kindness."

"You don't gotta! I would want someone to do the same for me!"

"No, I do! It just wouldn't be right if I didn't!" Amilia said as she really focused on the woman's pretty face and then asked, "Wasn't you just up there checking out that new iPhone?"

"Yeah, it's nice as hell, but I can't afford it right now," she admitted.

The young woman looked to be between eighteen and twenty-nine, and she wore baggy clothes that hid her shape.

"Well, I can, and since I owe you, I'll buy it for you. Don't say no because that would be disrespectful. Plus, I'm not from your city, and you're the first friend I've made. That's if you want to be friends?" Amilia flirted, holding her hand out to the surprised woman.

"Okay, yeah, we can be friends." She smiled and took her hand. "So, friend, what's your name?"

"Bossy! That's what my friends call me these days, but my real name is Amilia."

"Bossy, I'm Mimi."

"How old are you, Mimi?"

"I'm twenty-one. I know I look younger because I'm so small, but I'm really twenty-one," Mimi answered. "Bossy, can I ask you something that I'm not sure of?"

"Sure, ask away!" Amilia told her as they headed back toward the stairs.

"Are you into girls, or do you just hold all of your friends' hands?"

"Oh, I'm sorry. I didn't mean to make you feel uncomfortable. I just didn't want you to run off without me repaying your kind deed," Amilia said before releasing her hand. "And, yes, if they are as pretty as you. Is that an issue for you?"

"No, not at all! And thanks!"

An hour later, Amilia had the young girl looking like new money with her arms full of shopping bags when she dropped her off at home with the promise to pick her up later after her time at the gym.

CHAPTER 7

Watching You

The streets surrounding the busy east-side Walmart were crowded with cars as shoppers went in and out of the stores oblivious to Secret and Uriah sitting in a parked car with its engine running and the air conditioning on low. The two men were doing surveillance of the autobody shop where Uriah believed he remembered seeing the Escalade being custom painted. He knew if they liked the work that was done, they more than likely would return.

"Man, you do know this shit we on don't have anything to do with the owner of the Caddy. Hell! It's not even about them niggas. This here Amilia's got us on is personal."

"Secret, man! I don't give a fuck what y'all reason is for this shit! I'm just here to do what I'm told and show that I can handle whatever and still make that cash. I was pretty much holding shit down anyway. Jorge was always someplace trickin' with a bitch and gambling to do this shit right. He was big-headed as hell. To be real with you, big homie, if you hadn't given me the okay to off that fool, it was gonna happen anyway. He treated us like shit!"

"That all sounds good. But now who's to say you won't turn out to be the same way?" Secret asked, plucking the blunt out of Uriah's fingers. "Having money changes everybody in one way or another."

"I can believe it. But I love this shit, and I can tell it's in your blood too. Look at this shit! You's a boss, and you're sitting in this car strapped up on a mission with me."

"Yeah, I was right where you are now not that long ago, so don't think of yourself as less. Uriah, she made you one of us when she put that burner in your hand. So that makes you a boss in training."

Secret hit the blunt long and deep, filling his lungs with its very potent smoke.

A big red E&A-towing flatbed turned onto the block with the Escalade strapped to the back of it. When it backed onto the lot and the garage doors opened, they noticed the Infiniti parked inside already being worked on.

"Look, we got 'em! I knew they would bring them trucks back to this bitch to get fixed," Uriah said excitedly.

"Shit! We just spent all this time out here when that truck was already inside. We could've gone out and gotten an address on them niggas. Come on! Let's go see who will take a stack for the info!" Secret said as he opened the car door while still puffing on the blunt.

"I got a pillhead I fuck with in there, so we're good. It ain't gonna take all that," he informed Secret before he spotted Misty getting out of another car and walking inside. "Hold up! There goes that bitch that was driving it in the video. Let's go snatch her ass up!"

"Whoa, lil' homie. We ain't running in there and doing that shit in front of everybody. Let's just follow her and see where she goes. Didn't you say y'all had some kinda issue with her guy? We can follow her, get at him, and then send a message that we ain't to be fucked with!"

"Yeah, okay!"

"If these niggas are as tight as I think they are, that lil' bitch is the answer to everything!" Secret said, sitting back down in his seat.

Uriah agreed and then pulled out his phone and sent a text to Boots, his second-in-command, to get the soldiers ready to move when he had the information they hoped to get by following Misty.

CHAPTER 8

Miami Style

You could hear booms and screams all through the house as ETO and his younger brother Rules battled it out in a game of Warcraft in the back room of ETO's safe house. The place was also used to produce internet porn, which was Misty's side hustle with Rules.

Misty and her team of sexy females were in another part of the house setting up for a new scene while ETO's loyal soldiers were busy sorting and counting the money from his kush and gun sales.

Rules took a bathroom break from the game to relieve himself of the many beers he drank with his crazy brother. He was in mid-flow when he noticed that the house had gotten quieter. Rules listened harder, feeling something was wrong as he hurried to finish and get out of the windowless bathroom. He knew if the place was being raided, this was not the room he wanted to be in. Rules really didn't like being around all of the illegalness that his brother was into, but he loved his brother. All ETO asked him to do was to set up the video and lighting for Misty, in exchange for him paying for his schooling and the nice loft that Rules lived in off campus.

ETO was creeping out of the game room with his gun in hand when Rules walked out of the bathroom.

"What is it, bro?"

"I'm not sure yet, but I don't think it's the police. You get someplace safe, and as soon as you can, get the fuck outta here! Don't try to be a hero. This shit here is my world, not yours!" ETO told him.

"Okay, be safe, E!" he responded while jogging in a low hunchback toward the game room, which gave him the most exits if he needed one.

Boots and ETO had just made eye contact when a small gray canister was thrown through the window and started filling the house up with smoke. Suddenly, the front and back doors were kicked open by armed thugs wearing blue-and-black bandanas over their faces and yelling for everyone to get on the floor and not move. ETO and his goons went right to work with their guns. They fired at anyone that wasn't on their side of the house.

While they were upstairs, Misty and four half-naked girls and two men got to work trashing the computers and drives to their porn sites. Misty didn't think the gunfight going on both inside and outside of the house could have been the police, not when she could hear the sirens coming from a far distance. She rushed to look out the window and found out she was right.

"It's not the police, y'all, so get down there and help them!" she ordered the men. "Y'all follow me!" she then told the girls.

Misty snatched up her purse to get to her phone. That was when she noticed the woman sitting in a parked car outside the house with a smile on her face.

"Fuck!" she yelled, because her phone was dead as she led the girls down the back stairs toward the basement.

~ ~ ~

Secret and Uriah followed three of their men through the door. They were the only ones wearing vests in the group that started the gun battle. Uriah was rushed by one of ETO's goons and slammed into the wall. He broke the man's hold long enough to get his gun up between them and fire three rapid shots into his attacker's chest, which instantly killed him.

Secret was exchanging shots with ETO, who

looked to be already wounded by the way he was holding his left arm. ETO ran for better cover in the game room but never made it. The powerful slugs from Secret's gun sent him flying out the window he was passing. ETO died before his body hit the ground. One of the shots had hit him under the chin and exited out of the top of his head.

"Fuck this shit! Uriah! Let's get the fuck outta here!" Secret yelled as he rushed back out the way he came.

By then, the block was being stormed by MPD cruisers and SWAT trucks with their sirens blaring. Some were barking out orders for the few men they had cornered, to drop their guns and get on the ground. Amilia watched in horror when they took Secret into custody. But she knew she had to get out of there immediately if she was going to be any help to him. She drove away trying her best not to look like she was involved with the scene.

When she rounded the corner, she spotted Uriah dashing between some parked cars and into a gangway. She quickly went after him while paying no attention to the two men in hot pursuit of the young thug. Amilia slammed the car to a hard stop in front of Uriah, cutting off his path.

"Uriah! Get in! They got Secret!" she yelled through the open window.

When he did, she quickly drove away before the men could catch up to them.

"A nigga glad to see you! Them fools was on my ass, and I ain't got no more bullets," he explained to her, holding up his empty Glock .23. "We underestimated them a little. Shit! Who has all of them people in a safe house? But we would've had them if the police didn't show up so fast."

"What you gonna do now?" Amilia asked, slowing down to match the flow of the cars around her on the expressway.

"We gotta get Secret a lawyer, for one thing. Fam can't sit in there too long. Yeah, take me back to the post so I can think and have somebody go over there and be nosey."

"Okay, but don't worry about Secret. I got him. A lawyer ain't going to be able to help him because he's an illegal," Amilia assured Uriah that she knew what to do as she worked on a plan in her head.

Amilia believed that a plan she had worked out with Cheez years ago would work for Secret now.

CHAPTER 9

Blood Will Spill

The news of ETO's death hit his dear friends hard. Misty had found out from Rules when they ran into each other in the alley behind the house after they made their narrow escape from the sudden assault. Now Misty and the others were sitting in tears telling Trigga and the others the play-by-play story of how things went down.

"Dream, I could be wrong, but I could swear I saw that bitch your baby daddy had with him the one time," Misty told her between tears and fits from her broken heart.

"No! Oh my God! I hope it's not them. I don't wanna go through that shit ever again!" Dream said with clear panic in her voice.

"Well, if it is his people behind this, that bitch is on her own because Cheez is dead."

"How do you know that? Trigga, tell me how?" Dream demanded.

"I was going to tell you, but I didn't want to worry you—I mean, kick them bad feelings back up."

He walked over to her sitting on the couch with Misty.

"I didn't do it, but I had someone try to get me some info on him so I could handle his ass once and for all. But somebody beat me to it. My guy told me he was killed in a club shooting like a few months ago after that shit with us."

"But why didn't you tell me?"

"Well, y'all can work that out later. I don't know who the bitch is, but if she's the reason my brother's dead, I'ma kill that bitch and everybody with her!" Rules cut in, refocusing them on the days' events.

"Calm down, Rules! I know you're upset and hurting, but you ain't no killa. And I know that ETO wouldn't want you into this shit, so let us handle it!" Paper told him. "Misty, you said you recognized one of the niggas that was there too, right?" he asked, sitting on the edge of the La-Z-Boy chair across from her with Leslie sitting on the armrest.

"Yeah, Boots. They call him Boots," she replied, smearing more of her eyeliner on her face as she wiped away tears with her hands.

"Okay, this is the second time them niggas came

at us, and they took my brotha from us, so now it's time. It's our turn to get at them and end this shit!" Paper said.

"Misty, have you heard from Boom? We gonna need him and his guys, especially if it's them fools from down south. Cheez's bitch has a lot of power behind her because she's connected!" Trigga asked while holding Misty's moist hand.

She answered him and then handed him her phone, and then broke down crying even harder in his arms. Trigga held her for a few moments and then passed her off to Dream.

"Bae, y'all do what y'all gotta do and be careful. Les, come help me with Misty. She don't need to be in here with them," Dream said, taking charge of her distraught friend and leading her into another room so they could get her cleaned up.

"I don't wanna hear none of that shit you're talking about, Trigga. E is my real brother, my blood, and I'm going to get them for taking him from me, with your help or not! Y'all gonna have to kill me to stop me!" Rules told them with his pain clear on his face.

"Raul, please let us handle this!" Paper asked,

using the young man's real name, the way ETO would if he was trying to get him to listen to him.

"If it is them muthafuckas from down south, they might bright some bullshit here. They got issues with my girl and with all of us, and I'ma need somebody I can trust to stay here with them. Can you do that for me, please?" Trigga pleaded with the angry brother.

"We don't even know if it's the right people. Y'all both said it happened so fast, and it was smoky and there was a lot of shooting. So, there's a chance Misty's wrong. Stay here and let us find Boom and see what he has to say, okay?" Paper added.

Rules agreed and then fell back onto the sofa crying like a baby. They let him be and went and said their goodbyes to the women before going in search of Boom, so they could find some answers as well as send a message that it was not sweet and they would not be running away.

~ ~ ~

Three hours later, Trigga, Paper, Sam, and Teema were all strapped up and ready for drama riding in Teema's gold Tahoe heading to get some answers. They also needed to let off some steam because they were all hurting over ETO's murder.

"I know if we hit these punk muthafuckas the right way, they're gonna tell us everything we need to know!" Boom said for the third time while taking sips of the Crown Royal Black they were passing around.

"Here, bro! You need something to do with yourself. And pass that bottle, 'cuz I'm not running up in nowhere with you like this. Boom, my nigga, you need to calm down some, or it's gonna be a bloodbath with nothing to show for it," Trigga told him, tossing a sack of kush onto Boom's lap to roll up for them.

"I know you don't know how I do, but this shit here is my gas. I'ma show you. I'm good, my nigga. On everything I'm good!" Boom told them as he did what he was asked to do and broke down the weed.

Paper first looked at the men in the truck with him as they cruised toward the beginning of a war, and then down at the ring on his finger. He made a promise that this was going to be the last time Leslie and the others had to fear their past. He took a big drink from the bottle and closed his eyes for a quick prayer asking for their safe return. When he opened his eyes, they were stopping in front of a corner store.

The store was clearly a front for something illegal. The custom cars parked outside of it and in the back, along with the graffitied walls, told them they were in the right place. So they all took one last hit off the weed and drink, clenched their guns, and got out of the truck, leaving Teema behind the wheel for their quick getaway.

Boom was the first to enter the store, followed by Trigga, Sam, and then Paper. Once inside they spread out as much as they could in the small store. When one of the young hoods sitting on a crate saw Sam's gun in his hand, he yelled something in Spanish before he took off running toward the back door. Sam spun around and dashed back out the front to catch him before he could get re-enforcements.

"Take what you want. Just please don't shoot me. I have kids and I'm just an old man!" the well-aged Latino behind the counter begged, placing his .357 on the counter and holding his hands high above his head.

"Come from back there and sit on the floor on your hands, and you'll live to see them all tonight!" Boom told him, snatching the gun up while keeping his pointed in the old man's face.

"Where'd your lil' buddy run off to?" Trigga demanded, kicking the old man in the legs and opening up a bag of nacho chips from the rack next to them.

"I don't know. I just work here! He might be going to get help. I don't know!"

"Okay, pops. I believe you. Calm down before you pass the fuck out!" Trigga told him at the same time Sam was walking the youngster back in through the rear door that he ran out of.

"Did he tell you anything, bro?" Paper asked, after seeing the teen's bloody lips and nose.

"Nope! But I think I hit him too hard, because he forgot how to speak English!" Sam answered before he smacked the hood in the back of the head with his gun.

He didn't hit him hard enough to knock him out, just enough to ring his bell and let him know his life was on the line.

"Bro, lock that door. Watch him and make sure no one comes in. I'ma see if I can help him remember which side of the border he's on!" Trigga said, taking a spiked dog collar off the wall. "Let's take a walk out back."

In the backyard of the store, Trigga put the choke collar and leash around their hostage's neck and then pulled on it until it cut off his airway.

"Who ordered the hit on ETO?" Sam asked him, with his gun pressed firmly to the youngster's head while Trigga held the leash tight.

Trigga eased up the choke, and just like that the hood spoke English perfectly. He told them that he didn't know who or why it happened, but he had heard about it. He then said that he took his orders from a guy named Boots, and then gave them his cell phone.

"Now what do you wanna do with him?" Sam asked Trigga.

"We came to send a message, right? So send one!" he told him before he dropped the leash and went back inside to get Paper. "Bro, let's go! We got what we need from that punk!"

"Please don't!" the old man yelled, shielding his face with his hands, hoping they would stop a bullet.

"What did I tell you, pops? I'm not a liar, but you gonna have to take a nap now!" Paper told him before he knocked out the man out cold with a hard right cross.

As his head hit the floor, two gunshots rang from the back, and all three men came racing back to the truck. Teema smashed off as soon as the last one was inside.

"He tried to fight, so I had to pop 'im!" Sam told them before they could ask as they flew away from the scene.

What the youngster and old man did not tell them was that he was Uriah's girlfriend's cousin and the old man was their uncle.

CHAPTER 10

Stress Release

Amilia made two calls after she dropped off Uriah. The first call was back home to Webb. She explained to him what had happened and told him what she needed him to do. Amilia made sure to stress to him that it needed to stay between him and her, because she couldn't afford for her father to find out she was back in Milwaukee chasing after Dream again. Webb told her he would be there as soon as he could.

Amilia's second call was to her new friend, Mimi. She asked her if she could come over and stay the night with her because she needed a distraction from the worrying she was doing over Secret's arrest. Mimi told her she could, and Amilia headed back to the house she had dropped her off at the day before.

"I'm really glad you came, Mimi. With the day I had, I could really use a friend to take my mind off of it."

"Awww, Amilia, I'm glad you called. I've been

wishing you would since you didn't call me like you said you were last night," she admitted.

They were at Secret's place talking about anything and everything while doing shots of Patrón. Amilia had the TV on with the sound on mute, because they were playing the radio and she didn't want to miss the evening news. She was trying to catch an update on the shooting.

"You look good in that outfit. I told you you would."

"Yeah, I wore it for you since you made a fuss about it," Mimi giggled. "My cousin saw me with all of those bags and thought I found me a sugar daddy."

"Did you set her straight and let her know that I'm your sugar mama instead?" Amilia joked, laughing at herself. She saw the uncomfortable look on Mimi's face. "I'm kidding, girl. Relax!"

"Oh, okay. Because that's not how I see you. You were just repaying me for a good deed. That's all! And you're cool, so that makes you a friend and not a sugar nothing!" the young girl explained before she downed her shot. "And, Bossy, I really like you."

"So do you like me enough to help me relax? I mean really relax?" she asked the young woman as she moved closer to her.

"I don't know what or how. I've only kissed a girl before on a dare when I was playing a game of truth or dare."

"Did you like it?" Amilia asked, dragging her fingernails back and forth on Mimi's leg.

"I don't know. I didn't really think about it all that much."

"So you're curious? If so, I can teach you. Come on! It'll be fun!"

Mimi didn't know what to say. She wasn't sure if she was ready, but she knew she really liked Amilia.

"I don't know. Maybe after a few more drinks," she said shyly.

"Mimi, I don't want to push you into nothing. You can say no and we will still be friends." Amilia said as she stood up and walked behind her and began massaging her shoulders. "Let's take it slow. Just don't think about it, and give in to what you feel. When you say stop, I'll stop, and I won't be mad."

Mimi said nothing. She just gave in to her touch and closed her eyes. Soon the soft caressing hands moved down to her breasts, and her nipples stood to attention. Mimi was really getting turned on and couldn't believe it. Suddenly, Amilia tugged Mimi's shirt off.

"It feels better for the both of us without clothes on!" she told her before she removed her own top as she rejoined Mimi on the leather sofa.

"Fuck it!" Mimi stood up and wiggled out of her tight jeans and sat back down next to her teacher.

Amilia showed her how she liked to be touched after she got out of her pants as well. They did a lot of touching and kissing until Amilia felt the little quakes shooting through Mimi's firm body. That's when she pressed further and slid her hand down between Mimi's creamy legs and up her thighs.

"Mmm, yessss!" Mimi moaned, giving all the way in to the fingers exploring her wetness as they kissed and sucked on each other's lips.

"Tell me you want more!" Amilia whispered between kisses.

"Mmmm, yesss. More!" she replied, almost unable to get her words out.

Amilia was enjoying turning the young girl out so much that she forgot about the news. She then pushed her back onto the couch and kissed her way down Mimi's body until her mouth covered her warm mound. Then Amilia used her long tongue to work Mimi's clit the way she knew it would drive her wild. She moaned and bucked her hips as she came hard with Amilia's mouth on her and her fingers deep inside of her. Amilia laid back and went to work on herself when she was done. Her fingering parted her lips and went around and around her clit with her eyes closed. She was just building up when she felt Mimi's touch.

"Let me help! Teach me how to make you cum like you did me," she told her before she kissed Amilia, tasting herself on her lips.

Amilia pushed Mimi's head down where she needed her mouth to be.

"Now kiss it the way you were just kissing my lips. Let your tongue work the way you felt me doing to you."

Mimi didn't take long to master her head game. She sucked and fingered Amilia like she had been doing it her whole life. Amilia came for her over and over. They went at it until Mimi fell asleep in Amilia's arms with her leg wrapped around her.

Amilia must have fallen asleep herself, because

one minute she was playing in Mimi's hair, and the next she was waking up to Webb's ringtone.

~ ~ ~

Webb gathered all the things he needed to help Amilia and Secret as quickly as he could, and then found someone willing to charter him a plane to Wisconsin on such short notice. It would have been a lot faster and cheaper to use Mr. Gomez's plane, but Amilia did not want her father to find out where she was or that Secret had gotten arrested for something outside of the family business. Webb had to tell one person what was going on because he needed him to help him with Secret's escape. When they were about an hour out, Webb texted Amilia telling her he would be landing in an hour at Timberland Fields, so she would be there to pick them up. Amilia texted back informing him that Uriah would be there in a black Ford Excursion to take him to do what she needed him to do to free Secret.

Webb was a little disappointed about not seeing Amilia, so he sat back and thought of the night when he had watched her and Secret having sex. He planned to use this job she had him on to blackmail her into allowing him to have a taste of her pleasure zone and move him up in the ranks.

CHAPTER 11

What Am I Doing?

Uriah wondered why he had to use a black truck to pick up some guy from the airport. He hoped Amilia wasn't having him pick up his replacement because she felt like it was his fault that Secret got arrested earlier. This run made him think of how he got the position he held now. So as soon as he turned off of Hampton, he placed his gun on his lap to have it close at hand just in case the guy was his substitute.

"Yeah, speak fast, Bobo, I'm busy," he answered his phone.

"What up, man? I just found this phone, and I'm trying to do the right thing and return it to the owner. So if you know who that is, tell 'im I can bring it to him or to you, or you can come get it. I don't care. I'll even let you buy me a drink for my good deed," Teema laughed, trying his best to sound tipsy.

"Oh damn, man! I'm way out right now, but that's my girl's little cousin's phone. Hey, I'll give you twenty dollars if you hold it down for me for a few!" he bargained with the caller while turning into the airport.

"How long you talking, 'cause I'm not trying to be here until bar time."

"I'll be there before they announce last call. No, better yet, let's just hook up in the morning, and I'll give you forty dollars."

"Yeah, that's cool, man. But try to get up with me tonight if you can. I'm trying to party. Feel me, bro?"

"Just hold that down, and I got you on everything."

When Teema agreed and ended the call, Uriah pulled to a stop in front of the number 7 hangar where two guys walked over to him.

"Are you Uriah?" Webb asked, looking over the truck and nodding his approval.

"Yeah, you Bossy's guy?"

"If Bossy is the same person I think it is, then, yeah."

"She said I was picking up one person," Uriah told him as he clutched his gun, ready to shoot through the door if he had to.

"Well, I need him to get Secret out. Don't trip. I'll take the heat for him; but we need to get on the move, because this plane is rented by the hour and her plan only works if we get to him before they move him to county," Webb explained as he headed to the passenger side.

Uriah picked up his phone and texted Amilia to let her know he got her people.

"Get in so we can go."

"Who the fuck is Bossy? Is that the name the princess uses up here in Yankee country?" Webb asked once he was in the front seat beside Uriah.

"Yeah, something like that. I gave her that name," he told him, just as Amilia texted back. "Yeah, we about to do this? Y'all gonna walk in there and walk him back out?" Uriah asked as he drove them to the First District where Secret was being held.

"That's exactly what we're going to do!" Webb answered, removing two gold federal shields out of the dark blue bag that he had with him. "These babies here are going to help us do it."

He then handed one to his silent friend.

"What's up with him? Why ain't he saying anything?"

"Oh, Alonzo don't speak English. I brought him for show. If we're going in dressed as immigration agents, I'ma need some spice to make it right," Webb said with a grin as he passed Alonzo a royal-blue federal jacket and then put the other one on himself.

Uriah was impressed with how official they looked, and couldn't wait to see how things played out. But he still wasn't going to let down his guard.

~ ~ ~

Teema disconnected the phone from his computer once he had the information locked in placed to track Uriah's whereabouts through his phone. He was glad he was nosey and went through the boy's phone, or they would have missed it.

"So, you can track him to the exact place he's at right now?" Sam asked, sitting next to Teema's makeshift workstation.

They were all gathered at ETO's nightclub. They were in the back, but Misty had opened up for the night, saying it would be what he would want them to do to honor him. Trigga and Paper agreed with it because it was the space he needed to get all of their loyal soldiers and friends together to plan the next move.

"Yeah, look right here!" Teema pointed to a red arrow on the screen. "If we just wait, he looks like he's coming to us right now."

Sam traced the pattern in which the arrow was headed; and it if stayed on its path, it was going to run right into the yellow one, which was where they were.

"Hey, Paper, tell bro this fool might be coming to the club right now. See how he wanna play this shit!" Sam told him without taking his eyes off the screen.

"Make sure that's what's up, and try to guess what time he's gonna make it if you can," Paper ordered before he walked out of the room texting Trigga for his whereabouts in the club, so he could talk to him about this in person.

Trigga told him he was in ETO's VIP booth. Once Paper made it there, he saw that it was littered with flowers and bottles from all the people who knew him and had love for their fallen friend. On one side of the booth were Dream, Misty, Leslie, Dana, and two other females who were all engaged in a deep conversation with one another. Maybe they were reminiscing over their loss. At the other end of the booth were Trigga, Rules, Keyzo, and Boom, trying their best to blend in, when they were really scanning the crowd for hostiles looking to catch them slipping.

"Bro, Teema got this tracker up and running and says he thinks them fools are on their way here. So how we gonna play this?" Paper asked after pulling Trigga away from the others so he wouldn't alarm them.

"We good here. Real good because we know they're coming. But I don't think they're that dumb to really try to hit us right now. There's plenty of police riding through tonight. Just tell him to keep watch on them, and let me know if them niggas post up outside anywhere near here. I'll put everybody up on game out here."

"So what you think? They might try to make a move when we leave like they did before and try to get at us when the club closes?"

"Or they got a muthafucka in here right now watching us to see how we moving shit. Let me go put them up on game. You get them ready in back just in case Teema's right on the money with this," Trigga instructed him before he watched Paper walk off to spread the word.

Trigga looked around the crowd from where he was standing. The large mirrored walls surrounding the dance floor gave the club the illusion that it was way more packed. It also gave him and the others a view of almost every corner of the place, making it harder for anyone to sneak up on them when they were paying attention.

As soon as Paper returned, Teema told him that the arrow had passed them and was stopped at a police station on the south side. Paper still told them what Trigga said just so they would be on the same page if things changed.

CHAPTER 12

No Loose Ends

The MPD's interview room was small, clean, and cold. They had placed Secret there shortly after they brought him in and forgotten about him. He didn't know how long had passed since he had been in the room cuffed to the table, but it seemed like hours.

"Rise and shine, Mr. Sleepy Pants!" the hard-faced female detective said when she entered the room followed by her tall, cubby Latino partner.

Secret snapped awake looking a little beat and disoriented under the bright lights of the room. He pulled himself together and focused on the two sitting down in front of him. He smiled, knowing that they came prepared for his me-don't-speak-English act.

"Can I get something to drink?" he asked, deciding not to play with them. "And what time is it?"

"Sure, we can do that!" the woman nodded to her partner, showing she was the one in charge. "What would you like—a soda, coffee?"

"Water would be fine," he told her, reading her name tag. "Bells, where am I? Can I use the phone?"

"I thought we'd skipped the bullshit, Mr. Bermidez? You know where you are and why you're here. As for the phone, that all depends on how cooperative you are with us," Bells told him after her partner left the room.

"Well, can you tell me what you're holding me for or trying to charge me with? That's what I meant to say."

"Do you really want me to go down the list? How about we just focus on the three murders you're involved in, because the rest is just filler, to be honest," she answered, just as her partner, Rios, re-entered the room carrying two cups of coffees and a water.

"Bells, you seem like a smart woman, so I guess you know what I'm about to say next, don't you?" Secret asked, toying with her as he took a big gulp of the cold water.

"Me being smart doesn't mean I'm a mind reader, so you're going to have to tell me if you want me to know."

"I want a lawyer, please," he told her as he sat back down in his seat.

"This is your one chance to make a deal. Your friends in there are all pointing the finger at you. If I was you, I'd be trying to take it," Bells said, trying to get him to talk.

"Bells, he asked for a lawyer. That's it! This is over," Rios told her, reminding her of Secret's rights.

"Do you have a name of a lawyer you would like in here with you, or would you like us to provide one for you?" she asked while still fishing.

"If you let me use the phone, I can get you all the information you need on my lawyer."

Secret was only trying to get a call through to Amilia to tell her to go home to Miami. Because if someone was talking, she didn't need to be part of the conversation.

"Okay, well you can make that call when you're at county," Bells snapped at him before she picked up her yellow notepad and walked out of the room with Rios in tow.

Alone again, Secret put his head down on the table and closed his eyes and thought of Amilia. He wondered how she was holding up and if she had called her father like she did when Cheez got himself in a jam up here. Secret prayed she hadn't.

~ ~ ~

Webb and Alonzo walked confidently into the police station dressed as immigration agents. Uriah had never seen an immigration agent in real life, but they looked the part to him. Inside, Webb gave the lazy-looking third-shift desk officer his name and told him what they were there for.

"Are they expecting you guys?" the officer questioned as Webb signed in on the clipboard he handed him.

"They should have an arrest warrant right here for Bermidez. We got the call as soon as you guys put him in the system. I hope we don't gotta make this pickup harder than it has to be. It's late, and we just flew a long way and got a long drive back ahead of us," he replied, passing the clipboard back to the officer without letting Alonzo sign it.

"Give me a moment to talk to my sergeant. I don't think there should be any issue with you taking this one off our hands. I'm told he's not very talkative."

He let the officer go make a call to his third-shift

sergeant.

"Hi, Serg! I got two Feds here to pick up Bermidez."

Webb watched the officer's body language, because he couldn't hear the other side of the phone call. From what he could tell, it was going just how he thought it would.

"Yes, sir! They have all the papers. I'm holding them right here in my hands. No, I don't see anything wrong. Will do, sir!" The officer ended the call and then quickly made another. "Could you bring Mr. Bermidez up, please, with his things. He's being turned over to the Feds."

Webb smiled and then told Alonzo in Spanish that Secret was on his way out. Alonzo removed a pair of coal-black handcuffs from his belt and stood his full five foot ten, 235 pounds the way a soldier would when his commanding officer entered the room. Webb had promised him a job working for Secret when they pulled this off. Before tonight, Alonzo was just a driver for the Gomez family.

They didn't make Webb and Alonzo wait long. Secret was brought up to them within ten minutes and handed over by detectives Bells and Rios.

"This must be a serious dude for you guys to make a trip at this hour. I'm just glad he's going to get what he has coming from you guys," Bells said, pushing Secret into Alonzo's hands and helping him swap out the cuffs.

"Well, thank you for catching him. He's been evading us for years now. So you can imagine our surprise when the call came through."

"Yeah, well you three have a safe trip," she said. "See, if you would have just talked to me, you would be sitting in one of our cozy state prisons and not in the hell you're on your way to now!"

Secret just smiled as Webb and Alonzo walked him out the front door. He was glad to be out of there, but he didn't know if they were there just to break him out or to break him out and kill him. Secret was a little confused when he saw Uriah waiting out front in the truck.

Uriah couldn't believe his eyes when he saw the three of them emerge from the jail. He got the truck in gear and quickly pulled off once they were all inside. He headed straight for the expressway.

"Man, hell yeah! That's what the fuck I'm talking about. That's real boss shit right there!" Uriah cheered as he got them far away as quickly as he could.

"Webb, how did you find out they had me?"

"Amilia called and set this up. Man, I was scared as hell in there waiting on them to bring you out," he answered while uncuffing Secret.

"So how's the old man feeling about this? I know he'll want my head for this!"

"Yeah, well, you got to talk to your girl about that part. Boss, right now I need your man Uriah to find me a nice dark alley," Webb told Secret, nodding his head toward Alonzo.

"Uriah, you heard that right. Find us somewhere to relieve ourselves right quick like," Secret told him, catching on to what Webb was hinting at.

Uriah pulled off the expressway into a dark area by the lakefront pier and stopped. Webb got out of the truck and told Alonzo in Spanish that he should try to take a leak too because they wouldn't be stopping anywhere.

"They really had me stop so they could take a piss right now? They couldn't have held that shit until we made it to the spot or somewhere?" Uriah complained to Secret.

Suddenly, a short time after the two men walked off into the dark, Webb pulled his gun and shot Alonzo up close in the back of his head and then pushed him into the water before jogging back to the truck.

"Let's go!" he told Uriah once he was back inside.

"What the fuck was that about, Webb?" Secret demanded.

"Amilia told me she didn't want the old man to know about this, and the only mouth I can keep shut for sure is my own!" he explained with a prideful grin on his face.

"Take me home!" Secret ordered Uriah. "So where are you staying, or did you get a chance to get a room yet?" he asked Webb.

"No, I'm not staying. I'm just in and out. I need to get back home before they know I'm missing. There's a plane waiting on me that I need to be getting back to. You should let him run me there first."

"Whose plane did you use to get here?" Secret questioned as he powered up his cell phone so he could send Amilia a text to let her know he was out and with Uriah.

"I found a drunk white dude at the airport. Don't worry. I know better than to use the Gomezes' plane or anyone they know."

Secret thought about what Webb said earlier when he mentioned that his mouth was the only one he could control. There was something in the way he said it and the way Webb was acting that made Secret make the decision that Webb wouldn't be making that flight back.

"Say, Uriah. I need you to give our friend here the Jorge experience before we go!" Secret said, making eye contact with him in the rearview mirror. "Since we're pressed for time, the quicker, the better."

"I got you!"

Before Webb could protest, Uriah quickly drew his gun and shot him twice, once in the chest and again in the side of his head, staining the tinted glass with his blood.

"I hope that's what you meant, because it's too late now, boss!" Uriah said without slowing down the truck.

"It's exactly what I meant. Now get us someplace

so we can torch this truck and get home. Hey, when you picked them up, did you see the pilot they used?"

"Yep, you want me to take care of him too?"

"Not like that. Just take him some cash. Make it enough to make him smile and send him on his way. If he asks about them, tell him they're staying the weekend or some shit," Secret told him as he read Amilia's response to his text that was followed by a sexy shot of her kissing a pretty girl in his bed. "Nigga, you gotta hurry up and get me home!" he said excitedly.

Uriah got about seven blocks away from where he had left his car parked and pulled into an open field, where they gathered the things they needed out of the truck. Uriah stripped Webb of anything he had that was of value. He felt it was owed to him for the loss of the truck. Uriah was just about to set the fire when he noticed one of his cell phones was missing. He found it where it had fallen under the seat and most likely died from all of the missed calls. Now that he had everything, he lit the truck up and walked off.

"Please tell me why we can't call somebody to just come get us?"

"Uriah, the less people who know, the better. Like that shit with them that got me out. If Webb wouldn't have said what he was saying, he might be still living right now. But I knew I could only trust him in front of me because his words didn't match his smile.

"So I guess I'm good with you, right?" he asked, keeping pace with Secret as they walked back to the car.

"Why would you ask me that? What did you do?" Secret slowed down and readied the gun he had taken off of Webb that he had in his jacket pocket.

"You got locked up!"

"Man, that wasn't on you. Shit happens. I went right when I should've gone left. We good," Secret told him, relaxing his grip on the gun.

"Well, that's good to hear! A nigga thought that them fools was here to replace me or some shit," he admitted, pressing the remote start on his Acura.

Uriah plugged his phone into the charger as soon as he was in the car, and powered it up. It quickly started vibrating with all of the missed calls and unread texts. Most of them were from Eve. He didn't call her because he didn't want to be arguing with her in front of Secret.

"You ain't gonna call her back?"

"Nope. I'ma just go over there and face the music in person," he replied as he pulled onto the street to take Secret home.

There was no other conversation the rest of the way, other than the two of them making plans to hook up with each other later that day. When Uriah made it to Eve's house, she wasn't there, so he took the time to read her texts. It was at that time he found out that her cousin was killed and her uncle was in the hospital because he had a stroke after being knocked out. Uriah didn't bother changing out of the smoky clothes he was wearing. He just hurried back out the door and headed toward the hospital mentioned in the texts.

CHAPTER 13

Blowing Off Steam

In the back of ETO's nightclub, there was a lounge area that he made just for his men when they had their meetings. That's the place where many of them were gathered mourning the loss of their leader and friend while at the same time adding security to the club for the night.

Rules stood leaning against a wall in the corner nursing a drink in his hand. His heart was hurting, and he had his head down lost in his thoughts. He was bouncing through all of the stages of grief with anger fueling the burning need for revenge in his chest.

"Us having all of this info doesn't do shit if we're just sitting doing nothing," Rules complained as he walked over to Teema.

"I feel you, but you heard what Paper said, Rules. We really can't just go fucking with this nigga like that. We gotta do it right!" Sam told him while still watching Teema tracking Uriah's movements on the computer.

"Man, I just can't sit here! I need to do something!" Rules exclaimed as he walked closer so he could get a better look at the screen over Teema's shoulder. "Give me that address. The one where the punk started from. Y'all can sit here looking dumb in the face or come with me and—!"

"Come with you and do what?" Sam asked as he got up from his seat. "Rules, you're tripping right now, so chill out," he told him before he went out to join the party going on in the next room.

"I'ma take it to them. That's what!" he yelled behind Sam as he walked out the door. "Teema, you know you muthafuckers wouldn't just be sitting around if it was your brother they killed. Like y'all know if E was here, he wouldn't be on this soft-ass shit they on!"

"You're right, I'm with it, so let's go burn these niggers for ETO and the rest of the homies that were killed and locked up in that shit that day."

Teema gave in, and then he forwarded the address to his own phone.

"I got it on my phone, so let's go," he told Rules before downing the last of his drink and leading the way out of the club.

"Yo! What's up? Where y'all going?" Trigga asked, cutting off the three slightly drunk angry goons as they headed for the door.

They didn't know that Sam had already filled Trigga in on the move Rules wanted to put down just to make them feel his pain.

"We gotta go handle something right quick. I can't take all this standing around shit. Don't trip, but we ain't gonna go fucking with that nigga you got Teema watching. We on something else," Rules explained while slurring his words.

"Something else like what?"

No one answered.

"Look, Rules! I'm on whatever you on, but we gotta do this shit the right way. We can't be running up on them niggas all in our feelings and shit. Trust me when I say a nigga can't think straight when he's drunk and running off of emotions. And it's not like we don't know them fools got shooters. So tell me what is the three of y'all gonna do right now besides get killed?"

"I said we got this. If my brother—!"

"If ETO was here, he wouldn't let you do no dumb-ass shit like you trying to do now. If my nigga was here right now, it wouldn't be just the three of you going out on something like this. I know your brother. We been through some real shit together, Rules. So let's just chill and make a plan. Take the rest of the night to get our minds right, and then hit whatever spot you got on your mind right now when we know what we're walking into."

Rules reluctantly agreed and then allowed Trigga to walk him back to the booth with the others. Teema spun right around and went into the back so he could get back to watching the arrow. He was glad that Trigga showed up when he did, because he really didn't want to go at the unknown men without real backup, but he wasn't about to let Rules go and try to get at them alone. Once Teema was back at his computer, he sent Trigga a text telling him not to let Rules go anywhere alone, because he still believed he would try to go out and get revenge on his own. Trigga responded saying that he got him.

~ ~ ~

Amilia eased away from her lovers and sat up covered in sweat from their sex games. She sat at the foot of the bed while Secret was still pumping in and out of Mimi with her legs pinned over his shoulders.

Her moans of passion from the sweet pain he was giving her filled the room. She clawed and clasped the bed sheets as her eyes rolled when her orgasm came gushing down. He followed coming right behind her. Secret pulled out of her wetness and let his release cover Mimi's belly and breasts as Amilia watched and enjoyed the show.

"Hey, what are you doing down there?" Mimi asked her, wiping herself off with the soiled sheets after Secret left her to go to the bathroom.

"I'm just taking a break. Y'all are too much!" Amilia answered, accepting her kisses on her neck and shoulder.

"Hey, that's Rahji!"

"Are you sure?" Amilia asked, holding Secret's phone up so Mimi could have a better look at the photo.

"Yeah, that's her!"

"Where do you know her from?"

"Oh, from my job. I work at Ness's childcare. Rahji is in the classroom next to mine. She's like a little helper around there," Mimi explained while standing in front of her.

"Bossy, how do you know her?"

"She's my son's sister. Actually his half-sister," she answered honestly.

"What's going on with my phone?" Secret asked curiously when he re-entered the room and found them huddling over his cell.

"She works with Rahji, papi. Can you believe it?" Amilia told him, with her voice full of malice.

"I was just wondering if there was something more than good pussy with you," he said with a smile. "How did you get the job? Are you related to them or anything?" he asked, closing the gap between him and Mimi.

"No, I just work there part-time. Can we talk after I use the bathroom?" Mimi inquired as she rushed into the bathroom before they could answer.

"Now, how do you wanna play this? She's your friend."

"Friend? The bitch is just something to play with. Use her however you need to so we can end this and go home. I'm only here for one thing—and one thing only," Amilia cooed as she lightly took hold of Secret's length while stroking it in her small, soft hand. "You're all the friendship I need!" she told him before she wrapped her lips around his manhood and worked on sucking him hard again.

"Whoa, okay! But I still wanna lay low for a few days," he told her, pushing Amilia back down on the bed. "I need to make sure we can still move through the streets freely, because them punk-ass detectives were really on me. I need to get you home safe in the end, remember that."

They heard Mimi calling out to them from the bathroom doorway asking if either of them wanted to take a shower with her. They both smiled as they went to go join the naïve girl together. Amilia could not believe her luck and was already re-plotting her next moves. The thought of hurting Dream was enough to make her cum, but she wanted to have her man deep inside of her and her face buried between Mimi's legs when she did so. But Amilia held back until she was in the shower with them.

~ ~ ~

Rahji woke up right on time. She rolled out of bed, and then she and her little four-legged buddy made their way down into the kitchen where she heard her mother's voice as she worked on making breakfast. When Rahji walked into the room, she saw Rules giving himself a shot in his stomach with a needle.

"How can you do that? I don't like shots."

"I don't like them either, but it's something that I gotta do or I'll be sick," he explained as he finished and then put away his insulin injector pen.

"Oh no, no, no! I know you not in here talking to people without brushing your teeth and washing your little dirty face, princess. You know your mother told you to go do it, so go back and handle that and then come down for breakfast," Trigga corrected her and sent Rahji back into the bathroom.

Trigga had easily slipped into the role of step-daddy with the little girl.

"Yeah, Rules, should you have been drinking like that last night?" Misty asked from her place at the table, sipping on a hot cup of coffee while Trigga and Dream prepared to fix them all breakfast. "You don't be doing stupid shit, Rules. I need you!"

"I'm okay. I got this, and I'm here for you, sis. It's gonna be all right."

Trigga walked over to him on his way to the refrigerator and quietly told him that Teema had a good lead for them that he'd be following up on later that day.

"Him and Paper been at it all morning. They called all of us to meet up with them at the club so we can all be on the same page and handle shit the right way," he said as he pulled the door open. "You sure you gonna be ready for this, or was that just the drunk talking last night? It's okay if you wanna sit it out."

"Trigga, I wasn't that fucked up last night. I know what I was on then, and I'm still on it now. This shit here don't stop me. I'm doing this for my brother, so ready or not I gotta do it!" Rules told him sincerely.

Trigga knew that nobody went through the stages of grief the same way. Some went through all of the stages, while some got stuck. Some went through them more than once, because there was no real set way to grieve. But knowing you got some revenge for the ones you love made it a bit easier for a thug.

"Hey, why don't you two get outta here and let us do this since y'all wanna be over there whispering. Go on! Get out!" Dream said, taking the eggs out of Trigga's hands and then walking back over to the stove.

Trigga made sure Rules knew that nothing would

be going on until after the funeral. Because he wanted to try to make that day as peaceful as he could for everybody. It was bad enough they had to deal with all the drama that they didn't understand.

CHAPTER 14

You Asked for This

Mika's Style & Beauty was closed for the night, but open to Wicked, who sat talking with his cousin, Mika, the owner of the place. She had attended ETO's funeral service earlier that day and was telling Wicked all about it. Mika had no clue her cousin had anything to do with it. She was just spreading the hood gossip while cutting his hair. Mika allowed Wicked and his friends to use her salon after hours to handle their business for a nice price.

"Your pizzas must be here!" Mika announced when she heard the pounding on the rear door, knowing she wasn't expecting anyone.

"Damn! That's fast if it is! I just made that order like fifteen minutes ago. It might be Tony and them. He just texted that he was on his way here to grab something," Boots said, pausing his game and getting up to answer the door.

"I don't see nobody out there. So, yeah, it might be his playful ass," Wicked said after glancing at the surveillance screen behind Mika. "Tell him to stop fucking around, because the next time we can't see him, he ain't getting in," he told Boots before he put his head back so Mika could get back to his shave.

When Boots got to the door, he asked who was there. He didn't get an answer, so he asked again and waited. This time there was a bang on the door again.

"Nigga, I hear you knocking, but you can't come in. I hear ya knocking, but you can't come in. Ohhh nooooo!" Boots sang aloud and laughed as he unlocked the door.

With a bang, the door flew back at Boots, who stumbled backward as broken metal lock pieces and wood from its frame flew everywhere. Trigga exploded through the door, beating Boots in the face and head with the butt of his gun before he could recover.

Paper, Teema, Sam, Rules, and two others then quickly poured in behind Trigga, barking orders and waving guns at the startled unsuspecting men inside the salon.

"Don't fucking move!" Paper yelled, turning his back on a dark room to his right.

"Stop!" Sam shouted at the same time, squeezing the trigger of his riot pump and blowing the creeper that tried to rush Paper back into the darkness of the room out of which he came.

Trigga dropped Boots and then rushed over and pushed Mika out of his way to get to Wicked in the chair. Wicked started to reach for his gun but dropped the thought when Rules's gun was pointed three inches from his head.

"Hey, hey! Okay! What do y'all want?" Wicked said as he surrendered his gun.

He then looked over to Boots for what to do and shook his head for Mika not to get up from the floor where she had fallen when Trigga shoved her out of his way.

"Hey, man, we can do whatever. Just let her go. She don't got shit to do with nothing!" Wicked plead for his cousin's life, knowing it wasn't going to end well for them, because nobody was wearing mask.

"Bitch, get in the corner and face the wall! And stay sitting down!" Rules ordered Mika, making the decision for Trigga to let her live.

Trigga snatched Wicked out of the barber chair by his shirt and stripped the gun from his belt. He then punched him hard in the forehead two times.

"Let's not play games, nigga! Who sent y'all

after my brother?" Rules demanded, getting up in Wicked's face while pressing the gun hard onto the dazed thug's temple.

"Chill, bruh! I got this backup!" Trigga barked at Rules, hating that he disclosed to Wicked that ETO was his brother. Trigga knew how Wicked knew he would be a fool to think he could make a deal for his life. "Who's the bitch that sent y'all at him and why? If you tell me, I'll let you live as a cripple; if you don't, I won't hold him back anymore. This is where you start making wise decisions for your life."

Wicked thought of what Boots said about Tony being on his way there to pick something up. He prayed his homie wasn't too far away, so he started talking. Wicked rambled on as long as he could while praying for someone to walk through the door and save them.

Paper had Boots pinned to the floor under his black ACG boots. As Paper stood on the man's chest, he asked him all the same line of questions. He also made sure to keep Boots looking up at the barrel of his gun.

"Look, bruh! I don't know her. All I know is Uriah calls her Bossy, and that she fucks the boss," he told Paper.

Boots was now also praying for Tony to save them.

"Who's the boss? What's his name?" Paper demanded, pressing harder on his chest.

"Secret! Secret is the boss! That's all I know. Please don't shoot me! That's everything I know. If you let me go, I promise you'll never see me again," Boots pleaded, with tears running down his face.

Once Trigga felt they had all they were going to get out of them, he turned to Rules and asked him how he wanted to proceed.

"Fuck their life! Don't none of these bitch-ass niggas need to live," Rules answered right before he shot Wicked seven times.

Paper then put a bullet into Boots's head. Teema shot Mika execution style and then set a fire just because before running out to join the others. He jumped into the truck with Rules, and they all raced away, passing a few police squads as they turned off the block.

CHAPTER 15

Can This Be True?

The next morning at the safe house, Uriah, Secret, and Amilia sat listening to Tony and Jon as they tried to explain how they got sidetracked on their way to the salon. It was the one place where their showing up could have stopped everyone inside from being murdered before the place was set afire.

Uriah was already in a bad mood because he had to help his girlfriend bury another member of her family in less than a month. It was that and all of the stuttering that caused him to suddenly reach out and grab Tony. He pulled him to his chest so Tony could see his eyes.

"Nigga, you're blabberin' too much. I don't believe shit you're saying. None of it," Uriah screamed as he let him go with a hard shove. "Tee, you got like fifteen seconds to get the fuck outta my face!"

He drew his gun to let him know how serious he was being about the time he had given him.

"Naw, bro. I'm not—!"

Tony stopped talking when Uriah took aim at his face. Tony shook his head and slowly turned to leave, not believing how he was being treated by his homie.

"I should've known you was gonna be like them."

"Yeah, whatever! Time up, punk!"

Tony took a quick glance over his shoulder and then made a dash toward the door. Uriah's shots caught him in the back before he made it out. Instead, Tony stumbled to his death.

"Fuck!" Jon cursed at the sight of his friend being killed a few feet away from him.

"Jon, did I make myself clear just now, or do you need another example of what happens when I don't trust you anymore?" Uriah asked, turning his gun on the shocked thug.

"No, sir! No, we good. I understand," Jon replied in fear, not wanting to be the next to die over the lie Tony had old.

The truth was they were messing with some females they had met on the way to the salon, which is what made them late. Jon knew if Tony had just told them the truth, he would still be alive right now.

"Clean that up and then get back here. We got

some business to handle that's going to put an end to all of this bullshit so we can get back to business the right way," Secret ordered Jon before he turned to Uriah. "Are you good now, nig, 'cuz I don't think you are."

"Yeah, I'm straight."

"Yeah right," Amilia said.

"Just go home, and I'll text you when we ready to make that move. I need your head in this shit not worrying about shit else. You the only nigga I trust with Bossy's life besides me, so go get right as you can get, and we'll hit you when we ready," Secret promised.

Uriah looked over at Amilia and saw her nodding her head in agreement with what he had been told. He then promptly turned and headed out of the house, stepping over the big blood spot left on the green-and-white tiled floor to get out of the door.

"Papi, do you think he's gonna be good? Because I don't wanna do this without him?" Amilia asked while walking up and standing next to her man.

"Good for us, yeah; but for another muthafucker, hell no. I feel sorry for them, and shit ain't even went down yet," Secret answered, placing his arm around her shoulder and steering her away from the mess that Uriah made in the kitchen.

He did this so their men could get it cleaned up without the pressure of being watched after witnessing the harshness the homie dealt over a little lie.

~ ~ ~

Once she arrived at work the following Monday, Mimi decided to do a little more to help Amilia see Rahji, not knowing the real relationship between the two of them. So after texting Amilia the way she was asked to, Mimi also took the little girl outside to help her set up the recreation area for the smaller children at the center. It was still pretty early, so many of the kids were still sleeping, but many of them were up cranky and restless.

While outside, Mimi spotted her friend and waved in the midst of playing a game of kickball with Rahji and a few other kids. Mimi called a timeout when she heard Amilia's ringtone play on her phone, which alerted her that she was being texted.

"Can you keep her outside later than the rest of them? I don't want anyone to tell her mother that I let these two see each other," Amilia texted, making sure to let Mimi see the kid she had in the car with her and knowing she would think he was her son.

"OMG, he is soooo cute. IDK, I'll try. Wait, they just told her teacher that Rahji would still be here late tonight. I'll text you when it's clear for you to come back, okay?"

"Okay. How many of the teachers will be there?"

"There's never more than three of us here after hours. Like I said, Rahji is like our little helper since she's related to the bosses."

"Alright, text me then and don't tell her. I want it to be a surprise for her as well," Amilia reminded Mimi.

Before ending the text, she also asked Mimi if she was coming over to spend the night with her because she was going to be all alone. That was a lie to keep Mimi from getting suspicious. If everything went as Secret had planned, she would never see Mimi again.

Amilia drove around the block where Secret and the little boy she had with her dad, along with a few more of her men, were waiting for them. She explained the change of plans to Secret as she returned the kid to his father.

Secret agreed with the change because he was not

really feeling the idea of running into the center and frightening a bunch of kids to get Rahji.

He still wasn't sure about Amilia's plan for the child, after she had killed her mother. He didn't think she had the heart to kill a kid, but then he remembered all of those nights he came home and found Amilia drunk and passed out because of the loss of her daughter, so he didn't want to put it past her.

"Pull over! Pull over. Stop!" Amilia yelled for Secret to stop the car on their way back to the house. "I gotta throw up!" she told him, right before she opened the door and did just that.

"Ma, what's wrong? You good? Let me handle all of this shit. You just go home and get some rest."

"No! I'm alright. It's just something I must have eaten or drunk. My apple juice did taste funny, and I knew I shouldn't have finished it," she explained, not wanting to be left out of the action after coming so far and being so close to the ending of her nightmare known as Dream.

"Okay, but we're still about to go chill at the crib until she hits us later. But if I don't think you're feeling better, you're not going nowhere! That's it!

That's all."

Amilia agreed with Secret, and actually felt a bit turned on by the way he was talking to her. The way she was feeling reminded her of when she was pregnant, but she knew she couldn't be because the doctors had told her that her last miscarriage had done too much damage for her to carry a child again. But they did say that there was a slim chance she could. Amilia allowed herself to get lost in the dream of having Secret's baby for a moment.

"Hey, papi! Would you take me to a Walgreens or a CVS? I need to pick up a few things before we get to the house," she asked him, resting her hands on her belly and smiling at her thoughts.

When they arrived at the Walgreens on 35th and Wisconsin, Amilia ran in by herself, leaving Secret in the car talking to Uriah on the phone. She bought two pints of ice cream—one was butter pecan and the other was vanilla. She also bought two home pregnancy kits, a box of green tea, and a bunch of junk foods to fill the bag so Secret wouldn't notice the test kits. As soon as she made it through the door, Amilia went and hid the kits under the bathroom sink and waited for the right time to take the test.

Amilia and Secret spent the rest of the day in each other's arms watching television and counting down the hours while feeding each other ice cream. The tea and ice cream helped her with her nausea but did nothing for her curiosity. When Secret dozed off, she peeled out of his arms and went into the bathroom to take the test.

CHAPTER 16

Taken

"Say, Les, let me ride with you to pick up Rahji?"

"For why? So you can take another shot at Dana? That woman don't want you, man," Leslie teased Rules, even though she was happy to see him smiling like himself again.

"All I heard was hate," he laughed. "So can I ride or what?"

"Yeah, you're driving, Mr. Romeo," she agreed as she led the way out the door.

At the speed Rules drove, it didn't take them long to get to the center. As soon as they walked through the door, Rules ran into Dana, who was getting ready to load up the van so she could pick up and drop off some kids.

"Sexy, why don't you let me help you with them so we can get to know each other better? Just think, if you still don't think you wanna let me take you out, then you just got some free work outta me."

"Well, since you put it that way. Grab them two over there."

Dana gave in and allowed him to help her with the children.

Rules was so happy she said okay, that he took off with her with the car keys, leaving Leslie and Rahji stuck there until they returned. So after texting him a few choice words about running off on them, Leslie settled down with her niece and Mimi to watch *So You Think You Can Dance* reruns.

"Do y'all want anything from the kitchen while I'm up?" Mimi asked, using the errand as an excuse to leave the room after she received the text from Amilia telling her to let her in.

"Yeah, can I have grape juice and cookies please, Ms. Mimi?" Rahji sang as she flashed her you-can't-say-no-to-me smile.

"It's okay for her to have it," Leslie confirmed. "And bring some of them Fruit Roll-Ups. I need a whole box."

"Aunt Leslie, that's all you come here for—to eat all of the Fruit Roll-Ups," Rahji teased.

"Girl, shush! Ain't it past your bedtime or something?" Leslie joked, pushing her off of the bean bag chair they were sharing.

On the way into the kitchen, Mimi looked out of

the side window and saw Amilia's car pull up and park. So she hurried over to unlock the door to let them in. Mimi allowed Amilia, Secret, Uriah, and two of their goons to flood inside the center's rear entrance unnoticed.

"Hey, girl! Where is she?" Secret asked, giving Mimi a fake hug as he tried to see if he could spot anyone else in the place besides them.

"Rahji's in that middle room watching TV with her auntie. It's just the three of us here right now."

"Her auntie? Who's her auntie?" Amilia asked while getting in her face.

"Oh, Leslie. She's here. I didn't think you would care about her because you said for me not to tell her mother. I didn't tell Leslie either, so she don't know about your surprise visit either," Mimi explained, starting to get a bad vibe all of a sudden. "Bossy, what's with all of them?" she asked, looking at the men around her.

"Oh, they're with me. Who else is with her auntie? Did she say why she came here tonight?"

"She came to pick up Rahji, but the guy she came here with went out with Dana to drop off a couple kids. They just took off, so you still got plenty of time to visit with Rahji."

That's when Mimi noticed that Amilia didn't have her son with her.

"Bossy, where's your son? I wanna meet him."

"That's enough, bitch! Shut up!" Secret barked before he smashed his gun into the back of Mimi's head, knocking her out cold. "Keep y'all eyes open for whoever else the bitch forgot to tell us about."

"Papi, this is a good thing having her here. This way we can make sure there are no more issues coming up later," Amilia told him with excitement in her eyes.

"Yeah, well just in case, go back and get in the car until we bring them out," he ordered her.

Amilia knew it wasn't the time to challenge him, so she simply turned and walked back out the door.

"Hey, girlie! What's taking you so long in there?" Leslie called out to Mimi after hearing something bang on the floor from the kitchen. "What are you doing? You hand-making our snacks?" she said, not moving from her comfortable spot in front of the TV.

"We all outta snacks!" Uriah said as he rushed into the room with Secret in tow.

"What the fuck is this!" Leslie demanded while trying to stand up, but he was too fast for her. "No! No! Leave us the fuck alone! Get your hands off me!" she yelled while struggling with Uriah.

"Be easy, bitch!" he said before backhanding her so hard she saw stars.

"Where's Rahji?" Secret asked.

"Fuck you, punk! Leave!"

That's when Rahji walked back into the room and froze. "Let her go! Stop it!" she screamed, seeing the unknown man fighting with Leslie. Rahji had just returned from the bathroom.

"No, run! Rahji, run! You know what to do. Go!" Leslie told her, still trying to free herself from Uriah's hold.

Rahji quickly spun around and ran back the way she came. One of the goons stood in her path trying to cut her off, but she wasn't easily intimidated. Rahji paused long enough to kick him hard and fast between the legs before dodging his reach and getting away. Rahji made it to the back of the center, but didn't want to go outside at night alone, so she found a hiding place inside one of the large toy chests. She remembered the place from a game of hide-and-seek she had played earlier in the week.

"How you gonna get yo' ass kicked by a fucking baby? Nigga, you sorry. Which way did she go?" Secret scolded the man as he picked himself up off the floor after being kicked in the groin.

While Rahji hid waiting in the cramped box, she remembered she had forgotten to grab her phone so she could call for help like Trigga and her mother had taught her.

"No! No! You ain't taking me fucking nowhere!" Leslie yelled, fighting as they tried to drag her out of the room once they had her hands tied with a shoelace.

"Fam, just knock that bitch the fuck out so we can find that little girl. I know she's still in here someplace!" Secret told Uriah before continuing his search for Rahji.

Rahji tried to fight the urge to look out when she heard her auntie's screams. But once everything went silent, Rahji couldn't stop herself. She eased the lid on the toy chest open just enough to peek out, but that was also enough for Secret to locate her hiding place. He ran over and snatched the chest open, and then dragged the little girl out by her arms, kicking and screaming.

~ ~ ~

Approaching the center from the opposite end of the alley, Dana saw two men forcing a woman into the back of a big SUV.

"Hey, look. Something's going on!"

Rules had to break away from a game of peek-a-boo that he was playing with a little boy in the car seat right behind them to see what Dana was all excited about.

"Hey! Oh shit! That's Leslie!"

Rules pulled out his gun.

"Call Trigga and them now, and you and these kids get somewhere safe!"

Rules jumped out of the van and ran toward the truck to try to save his friend. One of the goons that was still inside of the center finished up the message he was told to leave for Dream. He then ran out of the center and spotted Rules running with a gun in his hand toward Uriah's truck. The man stopped and sent shots Rules's way. Rules returned fire from where he stood, because there wasn't any place for him to take cover. He had the man penned inside the doorway of the center until the second man sprung out of a truck not far from Rules and easily gunned him down.

All Dana could do was watch in horror as Rules was killed, but she did as she was told and quickly backed the van out of the alley. She hit a parked car as she tried to steer and call for help.

"Hey, girl, what's good?" Dream answered cheerfully.

"Dream! Somebody took Leslie, and I think Rules is dead. Send Trigga and them to the center now!" Dana yelled, half crying into the phone as she found a place a few blocks away to pull over.

"We on our way!" Trigga told her as he snatched up the phone from Dream's hand after hearing what Dana said over the speaker.

Dream remained on the phone with Dana as they all rushed over to the center. When they got there, the first thing they saw was Rules lying in the middle of the alley.

"Go check on him," Paper told Sam before he then followed Trigga inside the building.

Dream rushed over to the van as soon as Dana pulled up where they were.

"Where's Rahji, Dana? Where's my baby?"

"Oh my God! She was in there. She stayed here with Leslie and Mimi when I left to pick up these kids," Dana replied over all of the screaming and crying children.

"Rahji! Go look for Rahji!" Dream yelled, racing behind Sam in the center to look for her daughter. "Trigga, Dana said Rahji was still in here."

"Spread out and look everywhere for her. Rahji knows to hide if shit like this happens!" he ordered Paper and Sam.

"Aww fuck! Forget it, y'all! They got her—and Leslie, look."

After picking up Rahji's phone, Paper then informed them that there was a bloody note next to Mimi's dead body.

The note said, "Watch me!"

Paper pressed play and held the phone so everyone could see the video. It was mostly of the goons beating Mimi into relaying the message for Dream to come alone if she wanted to see her baby and sister alive again.

"That's not gonna happen!" Trigga said out loud. "We gotta come up with something else," he said while looking at Paper, because Leslie was his girl and he knew he wasn't going to sit this out.

"Hell no! That's not gonna happen. All they're gonna do is kill all of them when she gets there. As long as Dream stays with us, we got a better chance of getting them back alive!" Paper said, now thinking with a clear head.

"But they got my baby, and that's what Cheez wanted in the first place, remember? I can't lose my baby!" Dream cried.

"Dream, we not losing anybody!" Trigga told her while holding her in his arms.

"You said that's what Cheez wanted, but it's not what his bitch wants now! Because she asked that you come to her alone. That bitch wants you. That's it! That's all! So we can use that to get them back, but only if you don't freak out on us and do something stupid!" Paper told her. "Now let's get the fuck outta here!"

CHAPTER 17

Rude Hostages

Before Jorge was killed, he was having a shipping and receiving warehouse remodeled into luxury lofts. Uriah now owned the place, and it was where Amilia sat scrutinizing the child in front of her. She admired that Rahji was no longer crying even though she was tied to a chair in a place that she didn't recognize.

"Little Rahji, do you know who I am?" she asked, finally breaking the silence.

"You nobody but an ugly witch. Let me go!"

Amilia smiled at the way Rahji's face flared with anger the way Cheez and her daughter's used to.

"Did you just call me a bitch, little girl?" she asked while moving closer to her. "I'll slap your face for talking to me like that!"

"I didn't say that! I called you an ugly witch, and you heard me too. You just wanna hit on somebody because you ugly and mean!" Rahji told her, doing her best not to show Amilia that she was frightened.

"Do you know smart-mouth little girls grow up

to be home-wrecking little whores like their mothers. Like your ugly-ass mother," she teased before she suddenly got a warm feeling in her belly. "But that's going to change when you come live with me and your little brother."

"You're crazy! I don't got no brother, and I'm not staying here with you!"

"Oh, but you're wrong. You do have a brother, and you had a sister too, until your mother took her away from me," Amilia told her as she wiped away a tear from Rahji's face.

"Stop! Don't touch me! My daddy is coming, and he's gonna kill you and take me home!" Rahji yelled, trying to be brave and rebellious as she could to keep from crying again.

"What! That's not your fuckin' daddy. Your father is dead because of that punk and that whore you call your mother!" she snapped, flinching like she was going to slap her. "I'ma show you what happens to smart-mouth little bitches like you."

From somewhere in another room, Rahji could hear Leslie's screams as she called out to her telling her that they were going to be okay. The sound of her auntie's muffled voice caused Rahji to break down crying all over again.

"Auntie Leslieee!"

"Not so tough now, huh? Do you want to see her?" Amilia asked while squeezing Rahji's cheeks. "Your Leslie has a smart mouth too. I bet that's where you get it from. Yeah, I think you need to see her so you can learn about what happens when you disrespect me."

Amilia gave her head a little push, got up, and then walked out of the room, leaving Rahji alone again.

~ ~ ~

Uriah's goons beat on Leslie until she couldn't take the pain any longer and passed out. In her dream-like state of mind, all she could focus on was Paper's and her niece's smiling faces. All of the good times they had together flashed like a slideshow in her head, forcing Leslie to wake up.

"Yeah, that's it. Wake up, wake up! Waaaatch her now, bitch!"

"Get back! Get that thing away from me!" Leslie yelled, waking up to find Uriah standing in front of her holding back one of the big, ugly battle-scarred pit bulls only a few feet from her face.

"Whoa! Whoa now! Don't yell at her. Dixie Girl is sensitive to loud noises," he told her as he tightened his grip on the heavy steel chain.

Uriah continued to command the dog to watch Leslie, causing the massive beast to snap and aggressively growl and show its teeth. Leslie was powerless with her hands and feet zip-tied in place. All she could do was pray that he didn't release the almost two-hundred-pound, black-and-white, red-nosed beast on her.

"Please don't let that dog go!" she pleaded, trying not to make eye contact with it.

"Down!" Uriah commanded.

Although the dog relaxed, the beast never took its eyes off of its target for too long.

"Wow, you look a mess!" Amilia said as she walked into the room. "I want you to know, Leslie, that I never meant anything to happen to you. It truly hurts me to see you like this. Like, all broken and scared," she told her, wiping the bloody sweat from Leslie's face with a rag she had picked up along the way to talk to her. "I can make it all stop if you tell me where that bitch you call your sister is hiding."

"Trust me! Dream's not hiding."

"Okay, tell me where she is, and I'll not only let you go, but I'll also pay you for your pains. If I remember right, you love money, right?"

Amilia grinned and tossed the rag over to the dog to chew on.

"I want to see Rahji! I'm not making no deals or going anyplace without her," Leslie told her while spitting blood from her busted lips. "Tell me why you're doing all of this. We've been all the way up here minding our own for over two years now. So why start this shit back up now?" she asked, watching Uriah hand the dog off to one of the goons that walked in with Amilia.

"Why now? Now because that bitch took my baby away from me! She's the reason my family is broken. Dream has—!"

"Bitch, you're crazy! That's all Cheez's doing. And you're crazier than I thought calling that monster a baby. I bet he didn't beat and lock you up like he did her. Did he? And you calling that nigga a fuckin baby!"

Amilia punched and then slapped Leslie in the face, screaming at her to watch her mouth talking about her daughter. "You watch what you say!"

"She's not your fuckin' daughter! Rahji is Dream's—and only Dream's. As soon as you people get that through your heads, the better off we'll all be. This is crazy! Do what you wanna do to me because I ain't tellin' you shit, bitch!" Leslie screamed and then spit on Amilia's pant leg.

"You nasty bitch!" Amilia yelled, grabbing her by the throat. "I'm not talking about Cheez or Rahji! Fuck them! It's because of them both that my Adalin is dead!" she told her while still choking her.

"That's enough, Amilia!" Secret snapped when he walked into the room half dragging Rahji with him. "If you kill her, she can't talk, can she?"

Secret looked over and moved the little girl toward the enraged barking and snapping dog.

"Bitch, it's easy to play hard when it's just your life, but how about when it's hers?"

Leslie said nothing. She could see that Rahji was terrified, but knew in her heart that he wasn't going to allow the beast to harm her niece. So she said nothing and only watched in a silent prayer that she was right about him as he pushed Rahji closer and closer to the teeth.

"Stop! That's enough!" Amilia told him, as she

was becoming very emotional. "Make this bitch pay for putting this child through that," she ordered the men before she pulled Rahji out of the room.

Secret was right on her heels trying to explain that he wasn't going to let the dog bite her.

"I know you wouldn't, but she didn't."

Secret took Rahji from her as Amilia's tears began to fall harder.

"What's wrong with you? I thought you—! I asked if you was sure this is what you wanted, and over and over you told me that it was. So what changed?" he asked after locking Rahji in the windowless bathroom so they could talk.

Amilia seemed to withdraw, so Secret pressed her harder to talk to him.

"What happened is—! I'm pregnant!" she confessed in a low, soft voice.

"You're pregnant? How long have you known?" he asked full of excitement. "Why didn't you tell me as soon as you found out? You don't need to be nowhere around this shit here. You need to be—!"

"This is why I didn't tell you. I knew once I did, you wasn't going to let me see this through."

"You're damn right on that. Look at how you're

acting now, and that's my child in there, so I got more to lose. So, Amilia, you're done!" Secret told her while holding her in his arms.

Amilia apologized for not telling him. She told him that she still wanted Dream to pay, just not the way they were doing things now, because she couldn't stand how they were treating Rahji.

"I need to see if she's hungry."

"Ma!" he called as he stopped her from going to the bathroom door. "You know I gotta see this thing through now, right? These niggas lost too many people behind this, and there's no light switch you can flip like that just because you're emotional."

"I'm pregnant!" she corrected.

"I know. We're pregnant, and that changes a lot for the both of us, but this shit you had them start has to be finished. I'm sure your father has gotten word of what's going on here, and if not, he will soon. And I'll have to explain my actions."

He shook his head remembering how mad the old man was when he found out about Cheez having Amilia in the middle of his mess. The only difference this time is that he'd have to take the blame for her mess. Secret lightly kissed her on the cheek and touched her belly.

"Amilia, go back to the house. I'll keep you posted on all of this, but you know I can't have you here. Not now, right?"

She agreed and then pulled away from him to go see about Rahji.

CHAPTER 18

There Ain't Enough Room

Nessa had rushed to her place of business to deal with the police after 9-1-1 was called to try to save Rules. When the ambulance arrived, they quickly did what they could to stabilize the dying man. They loaded him up and rushed off to the nearest hospital. Dana rode along with Rules. She had to brace herself as the ambulance stormed through the evening traffic. When they came to a hard stop in front of the emergency room's entrance, the paramedics quickly rolled Rules inside. Knowing there wasn't time to stop and answer questions, the nurse ran alongside them to gather as much information as she could.

Trigga had started to head over to the hospital, but then Dream started freaking out with worry and panic for her child, so he turned around and took her home. The only way to calm Dream down was for Misty to slip a couple of sleeping pills into her drink. They were all feeling Dream's pain, but there was nothing they could do but wait until they had an address for their plan.

Once the distraught mother was down for the night, Misty had Trigga take her to the hospital so she could be there with her brother-in-law as well as give Dana a break. The doctor thought it was best to put Rules into a medically induced coma after the two-hour surgery, and the woman wanted to be there when he opened his eyes.

"Hey, bro! You good?" Trigga asked when he found Paper pounding the heavy bag.

"I can't lie and say I am, but I know I gotta be to get them back," he replied as he threw another fast, hard, three-piece combination to the bag, wishing it was the one that took the girls. "Still nothing good on Rules yet, huh?"

"Not yet, but he's a lot tougher than we gave him credit for. I don't think I could get shot seven times and hold on the way he is."

Paper stopped working the bag over and watched Trigga's face. He could tell he was wrestling with his emotions on the inside the way he always had. They were both broken over Leslie and Rahji being kidnapped. It was hurting Paper more because he now knew what he had put them through two years ago when he ran off with the little girl.

"Trigga, don't hold that shit in, bro. Not now. Like you said, we gotta keep our heads on straight so we can get through this shit."

Trigga wiped his face with his hand as he took a few deep breaths before sitting down on the weight bench at the in-home gym.

"For as long as I can remember, I've had like a block of ice on my chest to numb the pain in my heart. I never thought that pain would go away. But then Dream, Leslie, and Rahji came into my life and made me forget about it a little bit more every day."

Trigga looked up at the only brother he had ever known and saw that he wasn't the only one fighting back tears.

"We gotta get 'em back and end this for good, like I should've back then."

All the grieving thug could do was nod in agreement. What else could be said? He knew what was on Trigga's mind, and he planned to be by his side until the last body fell.

"Bro, we fuckin' trippin', fam!" Paper said, suddenly getting excited over something he remembered. "Let's go! We gotta get up with Teema.

That nigga should still have that phone tracking on his computer," he reminded Trigga as they rushed out of the basement home gym.

Once they were out in the car, they both got on their phones. One called Teema and the other rounded up the troops with a mass text telling them to meet them at the club.

"Hey, hold the fuck up, y'all! Y'all know I'm with you on whatever, but we need to rest. It's almost four o'clock in the morning. We all know what we gotta do to get them back. The best part is that they don't know we got 'em like this. So let's all go home and get some rest. If you can't sleep, take one of them joints y'all gave sis," Sam said after they found out the two most likely spots Amilia could be holding Leslie and Rahji from the app on Teema's computer.

Everyone agreed and went their separate ways until it was time to make a move on the two places. Trigga went home knowing if he did anything without including Dream, she wouldn't be quick to forgive him. So he went home and climbed into bed with her, knowing that's where he needed to be.

Paper went to his mother's house, the place he was having remodeled for him and Leslie. It was where he felt he needed to be, because it was where he planned on building his new life with the woman he loved.

Unlike Trigga, Paper knew he wouldn't be getting much sleep, not without Leslie or knowing that Rahji was safe. So before he took off, he had Teema upload the tracking program onto his phone. Paper didn't plan on making a move without the team, but he didn't want the arrow not being watched for too long. He sat puffing on a stuffed blunt watching the arrow that could be pointing to the love of his life, until he drifted off to sleep.

~ ~ ~

Amilia had given Rahji a big kid's Happy Meal to eat. Rahji knew her mother told her not to eat anything from strangers without letting one of them check it out first. The little girl remembered her mother really stressing that around Halloween, but Rahji was really hungry and didn't think the mean lady could put anything inside the chicken nuggets and fries. So she ate it very carefully. Rahji didn't drink the soda because she didn't trust it. She emptied it out in the sink, rinsed the cup out, and used it to drink water from the tap.

After another hour of sitting on the floor of the bathroom, Rahji got tired of being alone. She was restless, so she started trying to find things to do. She attempted to pull the sink from the wall, but it wasn't moving. That was when she focused on the heater vent. Rahji pulled off the cover and found that it was big enough for her to crawl through. She stuck her head inside and then went in as far as she could until she came to another vent cover. However, Rahji couldn't see anything on the other side while peeking through.

When she got ready to break through, one of the big pit bulls came sniffing around before it started barking like crazy and trying to bite off the vent cover. Rahji quickly backed out and put the cover back on the best she could, with her heart pounding from the sight of the dog. She got it together just in time before Secret burst open the door to check up on her.

CHAPTER 19

Because of Love

"Sis, you look like you're in love or something. Is there something I should know about here?" Dream asked while wiping sweat from her neck and face.

"Girl, I don't know what I'm doing. But it feels good to be with Paper. He's just so different. He has that thug-type demanding swagger, but he isn't really thuggish. I like it!" Leslie's face flushed as she talked about her feelings.

Leslie reached over and pulled a black leather ring box from her purse.

"I don't want to be without you. I need you to know that I'm yours for life, through whatever comes our way," she said as she handed him the box without opening it.

"What's this?" Paper asked, smiling as he opened it up to look inside.

Suddenly the ring box exploded in his hands. Everything went bright as the sun. Leslie could feel the pressure from the blast over her whole body, but she couldn't move. Then came the voices in the dark. She allowed them to lead her back into consciousness, and when she opened her sore eyes, the first thing she saw was a big man grinning at her.

"Yeah, wake on up! It's time to get this shit over with," Secret told her, shoving a phone in front of her badly beaten and bloody face.

He was forcing her to record a message to send to Dream.

Leslie felt what she knew to be a gun being pressed firmly against the back of her head by Uriah.

"I'm sorry!" she started in tears. "I tried my best to keep Rahji safe. She's alive. I don't know where, but I know she is. I know these punk asses are gonna kill me—maybe when I'm done doing this for them. I don't wanna die! Not like this. Dream, please take care of yourself and Rahji when you get her home. Don't be that girl again. Help Paper. I love you so much, Paper. It's my thoughts of life with you that keep me holding on."

"Bitch, shut up with all that and tell them what the fuck you were told, before I pulled this trigger and do it myself!" Uriah snapped, pushing her head with the gun.

"Fuck you! You do it! Do it!" she yelled.

She was then whacked in the head a few times with the gun to remind her of how close she was to death. Leslie had delivered the message telling her loved ones where her tormentors wanted them, right before throwing up and passing out again.

CHAPTER 20

A Hunting Expedition

Hours passed before Trigga woke up in a panic because he could no longer feel Dream's body lying beside him in their king-sized bed. He threw off the covers and sprung up ready to go search for her when the bathroom door opened and filled the bedroom with light.

"Did you sleep okay?" Dream greeted him, standing in the doorway of the bathroom. "Now, before I kick your ass, tell me the truth. Did you give me something to knock me out?"

"Baby, I—!"

"I know you did, because there's no way I would've slept like I did, so don't fuckin' lie to me! Besides, I got a fucking hangover."

"You were freakin' out, and it was the best thing to do for you at the time. So you can be mad all the fuck you want, but I stand on it," he explained, getting out of bed and walking over to her. "Dream, you still trust me, right?" he asked while hugging her.

Dream took a deep breath letting his warm body

relax her some before she hugged him back.

"You know I do, but tell me before you do something like that to me."

"Had I told you to take them, would you have?"

"Yeah, once I knew what was going on with my baby and my sister."

"So the answer is no. That's why we didn't tell you."

"What did y'all give me anyway, and who helped you?"

"Just a couple of sleeping pills Misty had," he told her, releasing her to go into the bathroom. "I told her to do it, so you can't be mad at her."

"I'm not, Trigga. Y'all didn't do anything without me while I was asleep, did you?"

"No, I wouldn't do that to you. We just got a few things in the works that Paper had remembered we had."

"You talking about that phone number Teema and Rules were tracking right?"

"How?"

"I could've told y'all that had you not drugged me. It popped in my head as soon as you two said I couldn't turn myself over to them to get my baby back," she admitted while walking over to the dresser and pulling out a dark, long-sleeve T-shirt to wear with her dark blue jeans.

"So you were going to go behind my back anyway. Is that what you're telling me?" he asked while washing his hands before brushing his teeth after using the toilet.

"No, I just—! It's my baby. What would you do if she was yours?"

Dream hated her response as soon as she asked the question.

"Wow! Tell me how you really feel. Dream, I'm not gonna trip on that because I know you going through some shit, but, wow!" he said as he walked over to the door. "But I would do just what I'm doing right fuckin' now for my princess," he told her before he then pushed the door closed in her face as she walked over to him.

"Bae, I know you love her. I didn't mean it like it came out!"

"I said I'm good. Now get dressed so we can go get your daughter and Paper's girl back," he told her from behind the door.

Dream knew she had hurt his feelings. Her words

kept replaying in her mind as she dressed and went to go fix them something quick to eat. Cooking was the only thing she knew to do with herself, because Trigga was giving her the silent treatment on Rahji and Leslie. Dream knew how much Trigga cared for her daughter. It was hard for her to just sit across from him and let things be.

"You ready to go, 'cuz they pulling up?" Trigga asked after reading a text he received from Paper.

"Yeah, I'm ready," she answered, following him outside.

They only had to stand on the porch for a few seconds before they saw the blue-colored headlights of Paper's Ford F350. Trigga was surprised to see the truck being used for the type of mission they were about to go on. He was even more surprised not to hear him blasting the sounds the way he was known to do.

"Hey, did any one of you call a cab?" Sam joked out the window as Trigga and Dream approached. "Get in! I take you wherever! Get in!" he said from behind the wheel, doing a bad imitation of a Middle Eastern accent.

Paper was sitting in the front passenger seat with

his head down watching something on his phone when they climbed inside.

"What made you pull this thing out, Paper?" Trigga asked, tapping him on the shoulder to get his attention.

"Oh, it's not mine anymore. It's his now." He pointed toward Sam. "I've been doing a lot of thinking, and it's time for a real change, bro. So let's go get them so we can have our whole family together the way it has to be."

"Nigga! Chill out with all them damn questions and shit, before you make him change his mind on letting me get this bitch!" Sam scolded Trigga as he guided the big truck through the busy evening traffic.

"Okay! Paper, what you looking at so hard?"

"I'm still watching this punk's movements. He's been to the same spot like ten times, so that's where I think we should go first. Sis, did they call you or anything yet?" he asked Dream after answering Trigga.

"No, nothing yet. I'm not feeling this shit either! It's like this dumb bitch is trying to make me crazy," Dream said while checking her phone just to be sure she didn't miss anything on the phone in her hand.

"Hey, where we going?" Trigga asked once he noticed they weren't heading in the direction of the club.

"We going to my spot because I got everything we need there," Sam answered.

"Turn on some music. I don't give a fuck what! Just play something!" Dream told Sam once everyone went quiet in the truck.

~ ~ ~

Two SUVs loaded with armed, angry thugs pulled over and stopped up the block from a small smoke shop on 27th Street. The occupants of the lead vehicle were Sam, Paper, Dream, Trigga, and Teema. They all took a moment to survey their surroundings and wondered why Uriah would be making so many trips to the smoke shop.

"What do you think they're using the place for—a front to filter money through, or drugs?" Dream asked, thinking about all of the times she had driven past the business.

"Maybe, but I don't care what it's being used for. If Les and the princess are in there, I'ma tear that bitch down to get 'em out!" Trigga said to Dream, his first words to her in hours.

"It still says the punk is in there right now. Well, his phone is anyway!" Teema announced after re-checking the arrow's location on his iPad.

"Fuck it! Let's go have a look for ourselves. If he's in there, then they're in there I bet. We can get this shit over with. If he not, then I'm taking whatever's in there for our troubles!" Sam told them as he put the truck in drive ready to move.

"Yeah, fuck it! Somebody in there is gonna tell me something," Paper agreed. He allowed Sam to pull ahead with the rest of their goons in tow to the front of the building.

"Dream, when we get up here, you stay in here. I'll call you when it's okay for you to come in," Trigga told her just as Sam stopped in front of the building.

Paper was the first one out, with everyone from both SUVs marching in right behind him. They entered the place calmly and fanned out around the inside of the shop, so they would have the best chance at overpowering any of the guys in there. There were only three men in view inside, but they could see that there was another space in the shop in back where others could be hanging out.

"How y'all doing? Just let us know if there's anything y'all need help finding," a scruffy-looking thug said. He was dressed in a T-shirt that read "Make Da Hood Great Again," as he stood up from where he was sitting behind the glass counter next to a skinny stoner.

"Is there something special y'all need?" the skinny stoner asked. He stood up and moved over to the checkout to let them know he was the cashier. He then adjusted a colorful lighter display at the counter.

"Yeah, you can call your boss out here so we can talk."

"No fuckin' talkin'! Put your hands out where we can see them!" Paper ordered, cutting off Sam's request and drawing his gun on the workers.

"Let me make this all easier for us and cut through the bullshit!" Teema said, taking out his phone and calling the cell he had been tracking to see which one of the three it belonged to.

"Whoa! Hey, y'all don't wanna do this!" the scruffy thug said as a phone began ringing from the back room of the shop.

"How many are back in there?" Trigga demanded, already pushing his way behind the

141

counter.

Suddenly, the third worker went for his gun. Sam and two of his goons quickly lit him up with hot lead, sending his body crashing through the large display window as he tried to dive for cover.

Paper grabbed the stoner and forced him to follow Trigga. He then shot his buddy twice in the chest, knowing he didn't need him.

"Ain't shit back here but this phone!" Trigga stated after giving the space a quick search for someone hiding or any signs that Leslie or Rahji had been there.

"Y'all grab them lockboxes and that work and let's go!" Sam ordered the goons.

They had to move fast since 27th Street was a major city street and they were in the hood known as the Zoo. They had to get out of the place fast to avoid the police and the rest of the clique. They took the stoner with them so they could question him as they fled the scene of the two homicides they left behind.

"Sam, pull around back of that empty house over there," Trigga told him after spotting a vacant home with a garage.

They took the man into the garage to beat the

answers to their questions out of him before killing him so they could move on to the next spot the phone had been visiting more than once. The stoner told him Uriah had forgotten the phone at the smoke shop when he stopped by the drop-off and pickup that morning. That was all he knew.

"Well, we have the phone now. I can track all of the numbers in it," Teema told them to lighten the mood in the truck as they glided through the night.

"That sounds like it's gonna take too long. Is there something else you can do?" Dream asked, full of disappointment for not finding her loved ones on the first try.

"There are three numbers I see I could focus on that have a lot of back and forth between them," Teema told her as his fingers went to work on the keys of his tablet. "One of them is our next target too," he announced as he read off Eve, Bossy, and Secret's names.

"Secret. Track that one!" Trigga told him.

He remembered hearing that name before, but he didn't know where or why. But he planned to find out to get his friends back.

"Oh shit! Somebody's calling me!" Dream said,

hurrying to pull her phone out of her jeans pocket. When she did, she saw that it was a video message, so she pressed play.

CHAPTER 21

No Time for Panic

Amilia was really feeling good about carrying a child again. She was so excited that she walked around the house debating with herself about calling her mother and telling her. It had been awhile since she had spoken to her mother or her son, and she was really missing his little cute face. So with nothing to do and not wanting to call Secret to come be with her knowing the mess she had him dealing with, Amilia broke down and made the call to her mother.

"Ma, I did this in my daughter's and husband's name. I know this baby is their way of thanking me," she argued with her mother. "That little girl's mother had to be punished for what she did to my family, Mama," Amilia continued while rubbing her belly with her free hand.

"Oh, Amilia! You're not thinking of what you're doing with a pure heart. You have too much hate and pain there to think clearly. I want you to come home so I can help you. If you're pregnant, that could be a sign that you should stop what you're doing because all is forgiven."

"You don't believe me. Why can't you be happy for me! You took my son from me, and I'm not going to let you take this one. Just tell my baby boy that I love him and forget I called, Amilia snapped in anger because her mother didn't believe her and thought she was crazy.

After the call, she took a hot shower and then dressed in the pajamas Mimi had picked out with her the day they met. Amilia had to admit to herself that she missed Mimi's company and that she shouldn't have let them kill her. With a heavy heart and nothing else to do, she got in bed and buried her head under the covers. As soon as her head touched the pillow, she began to wonder how Rahji was doing. She knew the little girl was scared and alone, locked away like a dog. For the first time, Amilia realized how crazy it was for her to think that Rahji could ever love her after she killed her mother and aunt. Alone and feeling sad, remorseful, and guilty, she fell asleep.

~ ~ ~

Worried and excited about the idea of being a father, Secret broke away from Uriah to go home to check on Amilia. He didn't call first because he wanted to surprise her. When he walked into their place, all was quiet. He found Amilia sleep in bed, so he decided to take his little plan a step further. He hid in a dark corner and tossed a hair brush across the room.

Amilia woke up right away. She then sat up in bed and listened for the sound that woke her up. That's when Secret snuck up behind her and coved her scream with his hand.

"Shhhh! Don't do that. No screaming. I don't wanna have to tickle you to death," he chuckled. "If I let you go, will you play nice?"

She couldn't help but smile behind the hand over her mouth. She nodded, and he moved his hand away slowly just in case she changed her mind and screamed anyway.

"Ohhh, you got me started now. I want more, Mr. Bad Guy."

"Okay!"

Secret looked around the room until he found one of his white button-downs hanging on the back of the door. He tore the sleeves off of the shirt and then used them to tie Amilia's hands to the bedpost.

"Oh no! No! No! What are you going to do to

me?" Amilia asked, getting into the character of a helpless woman. "I can give you money if you stop this."

Secret didn't respond. He just pushed her head down, climbed on the bed, and straddled her legs. Then he teasingly ran his hand up her body, grabbing her by the throat with a pressure that made her cum a little.

Amilia liked the role playing a lot. She moaned when he ripped her top down the middle, which popped its buttons. Secret started sucking on her neck and then nipples before kissing his way down her body, until he stopped by her pajama bottoms. He took the time to take off his shirt and jeans, and then he roughly snatched off her soft cotton shorts before diving headfirst between her thighs.

Secret let his tongue work its magic on her clit as his fingers danced in her wetness until they were good and covered with cum. He tickled her asshole a moment and then pushed his cum-covered fingers inside. Amilia came hard, squirting her juices as she soaked the sheets. He continued to pump his finger in and out of her until he was too hard and awake to deny himself of her wetness any longer. Suddenly he pulled his fingers out of her and then tossed her legs over his shoulders and rammed his hardness deep inside on her.

He pushed her legs back as far as he could and held them there stroking Amilia fast and hard until he came. She held him deep in place while they kissed through the climax.

"I'm glad you came home. I don't know if it was the baby or what, but I really was missing you before I went to bed."

"I guess we were feeling the same at the same time, because that's why I came home," Secret said as he kissed her tenderly and placed his hand on her belly. "I can't believe there's a little me in there. I remember being so envious when you came home to visit your parents with your big ol' belly."

"Hey, you calling me fat?" she giggled playfully while hitting him.

"Well, you were all baby," he said while laughing and kissing the fight right out of her. "I wanted you to be carrying my baby way back then. He didn't deserve you."

Secret's personal phone started playing the ringtone set for the old man, and his heart skipped a beat because the old man didn't call him just to talk. There had to be something wrong. He jumped out of bed to answer it.

"Secret, don't answer it. It's nothing."

"Amilia, you know I can't do that!"

"I'm telling you that it's okay. I talked to my mother tonight and told her about the baby. She wants me to come home, and I told her that I wasn't because she just wants to take our baby away from me. She must've told Papa."

"Please tell me you didn't tell her where we were," he said, letting the call go to voicemail.

But when it rang right back, he knew he had to answer it.

"Not really. I don't think!" Amilia responded, knowing she had said too much when she got mad at her mother.

"Fuck!" Secret cussed when answering the call that could be the end of his life.

CHAPTER 22

We Coming for Ours

After watching the recording of Leslie for the tenth time since they returned to Sam's spot, Teema was able to do his thing and track its last known location. Now they were all getting locked and loaded to storm the place and bring Rahji and, hopefully, Leslie back alive. Trigga and Paper stood side by side loading extra thirty-round clips for their Glocks while Sam used his time to replace the factory stocks with bump stocks to make their semi-autos spray like full autos. Their anger warmed the air in the room around them.

"Hey, y'all, listen up right fast!" Trigga yelled, getting everyone's attention once he was all strapped up for war. "I gotta thank you niggas for going all out for us. I'm speaking for all of us when I say that. But this is it right here. By all means, I'ma bring that little girl home to her mother, and her sis back to Paper. If not, ain't none of the punks gonna walk out of there with their lives. I'm not gonna trip if any of you wanna fall!"

"If you about to tell us that we can go home or some shit like that, save it, nigga! We started this shit with you, and we gonna finish this shit with you. We all family, and we all need to get some get-back for what they did to ETO and Rules. That nigga is laying up fighting for his life right now. So we in it until the casket drops. So if you don't got nothing good to say, let's shut the fuck up and go handle this shit," Biggie said. He was one of the six other men in the room ready to put his life on the line for them.

~ ~ ~

Leslie was very weak from the lack of water and the beatings she had been taking. She could barely hold her head up and keep her eyes open because of the great pain she was in.

"Why? Why are you bitches still hitting on me?" she asked, with blood dripping from the two new cuts on her lips. "Just kill me and get it over with. Either way, my nigga's gonna find out and kill y'all and everyone you know. So do it already!"

"Bitch, please! Your punk-ass nigga, Mr. Super Thug, ain't coming to do shit. Don't no muthafucker know where your punk ass at. But if you wanna die so fast, do a nigga a solid and just stop breathing and die."

"Ohhhh, he's coming, and when he gets here, if I'm still alive, I'ma watch him as he kills you bad," she promised before passing out again.

The dumb goon slapped her back awake. He hit her so hard that her head snapped to the side like she was a rag doll.

"Naw, bitch! Don't die yet! I want you to live to see me kill your man if his corny ass comes for you, which he's not. I'ma watch you die slowly, waiting for him like the dumb bitch you is." He laughed before he punched her in the ribs for the hell of it.

Leslie was in serious pain, but she forced herself to look up and stare into the eyes of the guy who was beating on her. She silently prayed for his death while holding onto the hope that Paper and the others would come and save her.

~ ~ ~

Rahji was getting restless again still locked in the bathroom. It had been some time since anyone had come to check on her, and she began to wonder if they had forgotten about her. Her focus once again turned to the vent. So she crawled over to it and pressed her face to it, trying to see if she could see the dogs. She couldn't without going inside, so she removed the cover once again and crawled inside.

Rahji could see the dogs sleeping, and she could see that the door to their room did not have a lock on it that she could see. She wanted to try to check it to see if she could get out and find a phone to call for help. She remembered how she used to sneak away from Tracy without waking her up, so she figured if she could do it with a little dog, then she could do it with these big ones. Rahji pushed on the vent until it loosened enough to get her finger through so she could keep it from crashing to the floor when she took it off.

When she got it off, she paused to see if she had awakened any of the dogs. She hadn't, so she moved on, tiptoeing across the filthy tiled floor to the door. She then paused to check to see if the dogs were still unaware that she was in the room with them. Satisfied, Rahji then tried the doorknob. The lock clicked and the door creaked when she pulled it open, which woke the big-headed beasts. One of the dogs let out a menacing growl, but Rahji didn't wait to see what it would do next. She flung the door open and ran as fast as her little legs would allow her, hoping the dogs went back to sleep.

CHAPTER 23

A Mother's Love

Dream had a feeling that Trigga and the others planned to leave her outside in the truck when they got to the location where they believed her loved ones were being held. But she wasn't having it, so she dressed for battle just like the rest of them. Dream strapped up with two guns, a few extra clips, and double-plated body armor.

"How do we get in there without losing our surprise? Shit! We don't know how many in that bitch, so we gotta catch 'em off guard," Sam said once they were outside the building.

"I'm looking for a way now, but Wi-Fi is choppy over here," Teema answered, with his fingers working overtime on his tablet.

"Fuck this shit. I ain't waiting!" Dream said, jumping back in the truck. "Just follow me!" she told them, yelling out the window as she stomped the gas pedal to the floor.

The big SUV shot forward and picked up speed fast and rammed right through the door. Dream didn't let up on the pedal until most of the truck was inside the building. The force of the airbag hitting her in the face knocked her silly for a few moments.

Trigga was the first to take off sprinting after the truck while the others quickly followed with guns ready. Trigga made it through the hole Dream had made for them, just as one of the thugs inside was about to try to snatch her out of the truck. Trigga shot him and sent shots at the closest man next to him. Paper shot another in the face but was tackled by Uriah, which sent them both tumbling down a flight of nearby stairs. When they hit the first landing, they both quickly got on their feet throwing hard fists that were hitting each other wherever they landed. Paper somehow got off a brutal sidekick that sent Uriah sailing over the banister before he quickly ran back up to join the gunfight that was going on above him, before Uriah's body hit the floor.

"Watch your backs!" he yelled, pulling his second gun after losing the first when he was tackled.

Sam and Trigga were going at it hand to hand with some of the reinforcements that flooded in to see what all the shooting was about. Paper helped to clear the way by sending shots at the six thugs with whom they were fighting. The rest of their goons were trading fire with the reinforcements that were smart enough to take cover behind something in the firefight.

"Teema, which way to go?" Dream asked, hiding next to him and two of their goons that were doing what they could to keep her alive.

"Shit! This way, Dream!"

She ran off on her own, but he knew she would run off either way if he told her or not.

"Bigman, y'all two come follow us," he ordered two of his goons.

Teema led the way for them by using his tablet to go in search of the two they had come to rescue. He followed the blinking arrow on his tablet, which flashed faster and faster the closer they got to finding the phone with which the recording was made. They had to keep being redirected because of all of the remodeling that had been done to the building's interior. Teema was getting frustrated, so he rushed around a corner without looking and ran right into a few of their adversaries coming down the hall.

"Teema, duck!" Dream yelled, firing her gun over his head at the surprised thugs in front of him.

One of their goons took one in the neck and went down choking on his blood. Teema crawled over to him and took his gun, knowing the man wasn't going to make it out alive. Once Bigman let his fully automatic loose and Teema joined in with the one he picked up, the gunfight ended as fast as it started. Dream had to dive into one of the rooms for cover after she emptied her second gun.

"Dream? Dream! Where you at? You good?" the men called to her while reloading their guns.

"Shit! Yeah! I'm okay. I'm good! I just ran outta bullets!" she answered as she reloaded. She was a bit shaken by the close call with death, but added, "I'm ready to go."

"Okay, because I think we gotta go through that door at the end of the hall. I bet that's where these niggas came from," Teema told them. "We should call for the others and wait."

"Is you sure, or are you guessing?" Dream asked after rejoining them. "Yeah, I'm sure," he replied while looking down at the cracked screen on his tablet.

"Teema, they might kill them since they know we're here now," Bigman said as he also reloaded.

"Yeah, you should call 'em, but we can't wait on them to get here."

"Is that what you think too?" Teema asked, just to be asking. "He would be a fool to think she would say differently."

"I do. So you two got the big guns, so y'all need to lead the way!" Dream told them.

Teema shook his head as he quickly sent out a mass text of their whereabouts to the others. Then the three of them moved quickly but cautiously forward until they were standing right outside the door.

"Kick it in! Shoot everybody in here that's not them!" Bigman said while looking mostly at Dream, who had tears in her eyes.

He didn't know if the tears were from fear or anticipation, but he wanted her to be ready.

"Let's do it!" Dream told him after taking a few deep breaths and readying herself.

Bigman kicked down the door with such force that he fell inside with it. Teema watched it happen and rushed in, jumping over him and waving his gun, ready to provide cover so Bigman could get back on his feet. Dream followed, almost kicking him in the face as she did. The only person they saw inside was

Leslie.

"Oh my God! Leslie! Les?" Dream called to her beaten and bloody friend.

"Dream, no! Look out!" Leslie yelled, snapping back into consciousness just in time to warn them of the two men hiding.

Dream was already in motion when two shooters suddenly popped up from behind a pile of plywood and drywall shooting at them. Dream dropped to the floor quickly, returning fire along with the others. Teema was the one hit first. He went down hard. He was cussing, but he didn't stop busting his gun.

"Fam, you okay? Where you hit?" Bigman asked after sneaking up on the creepers from the other side and killing them.

"Aww shit, man! They shot me in my leg," he answered while grunting out in pain.

"Can you walk on it?"

"I have to. Just go help Dream with her sister. I got the door," Teema told him bravely, picking his gun back up and covering the door.

"Look at what they did to you. Oh my God! Leslie, can you walk?" Dream asked as she worked on getting Leslie's hands and feet loose.

"I think so," she answered, still fading in and out of consciousness.

"Les? Les, wake up! Where is my baby? Where is Rahji, Leslie?"

"I don't know. They got her out there someplace. That bitch Amilia. She kept us apart. I'm sorry, sis. I—!"

"No! No you don't. It's okay. Let's get you outta here. I'ma find her!" Dream tried to assure her, but she had passed out again.

"Big, get her outta here. I'm going to find my baby."

"No, Dream! You can't go nowhere by yourself. You see these punks hiding behind shit. No!" Teema told her, now back on his feet but moving with a bad limp.

"You can't stop me! I gotta find her, and y'all need to stick together to get outta here."

"Dream, I gotta carry her, and you see he can barely walk, so we need you or we're not gonna make it out of this bitch!" Bigman said as he scooped Leslie up and tossed her over his shoulder. "Once you help me get them outside safe, me and you right in this bitch until we find Rahji. I promise you that."

As much as Dream didn't want to go, she knew they were telling her right. She gave in and accepted his promise to come back with her. She let Teema lean on her and then followed Bigman back out the way they came. Once they made it to the end of the hall, they heard something that sounded like a dog chasing someone. They then heard a voice.

"Stop! Go away!" Rahji yelled, with the big dogs snapping at her.

The beasts were toying with her, but she couldn't tell the difference with the unknown animals.

"Hey, Big, hold up! I think I just heard her."

As soon as the words left Dream's mouth, Rahji came racing around the corner with two huge pit bulls seconds behind her.

"Hey, stop!" Bigman yelled, but it was too late. Dream had taken off toward her child.

"Run, baby! Run!"

"Mama?" Rahji cried, not believing her mother was there. "Mama, make 'em stop!" she begged while never slowing down.

Dream didn't know what to do. Her hand tightened around the handle of her gun, but she didn't trust her aim with her baby so close.

"Mama, help meee!" Rahji yelled, getting tired because she had already been running top speed for over five minutes from the dogs.

"Just keep coming!"

Dream took aim and just started shooting over and behind her daughter. The loud booms from the gun did their job, scaring the dogs and causing them to take pause. But it also did the same to Rahji. The little girl was moving too fast to just stop and fell hard only a few feet from her mother and the dogs.

"Get up! Get up! Come on, Rahji!" Teema and Bigman told her.

But the shock of the gunfire quickly wore off on the dogs, and they were now angry. Dream dashed the distance remaining between her and her child. She prayed that the others had her back if the dogs decided to try her. She dropped down and wrapped her arms tightly around Rahji before she scooped her up off of the floor and hugged her. The dogs growled louder.

"Baby, I need you to keep being strong for me so we can get away from them," Dream said, slowly putting her down without taking her eyes off the big beasts. "We gotta back up. Walk backward real slow, okay?"

"Okay!" Rahji said as she held her mother's hand tighter. "Can't you shoot them with your gun, Mama, so they can't get us?"

"No, they're too close. There are too many of them for us to get away in time," she answered, pushing Rahji behind her as they backed away.

Once Bigman saw they were far enough away from the dogs for Teema to cut them down if they decided to charge, he told Dream to turn and run.

"T, burn them mutts now!" Bigman told him, trying to balance Leslie's dead weight on his shoulders.

Teema took aim with the assault rifle that he was half using as a crutch and let it ride. Dream spun around roughly dragging Rahji as they ran. As soon as the beasts began to come after them, Teema's first few shots seemed to only enrage the dogs more. Then one went down from a lucky headshot, followed by another whining in pain from too many body shots before Teema's gun clicked empty.

Bigman was off running with Leslie. Dream was also running with Rahji in her arms, so that left him to try to keep up with them on his one good leg.

"Oooh shit!" Teema said aloud, looking back to see if the last dog was coming after him.

Two of them were dead, but another one had joined the third, and now the two angry beasts were gaining on him quickly. Teema looked back ahead of him and saw his friends all burst through a door marked Exit. In his best judgment, he wasn't going to make it out of there with them before the dogs caught up with him. So with all he had in him, Teema slammed his shoulder into the closed door closest to him and allowed himself to fall into the room. He then quickly kicked the door closed behind him and sat down with his back on it to hold it shut. The dogs went berserk barking and ramming the door, trying to get at him. All Teema could do was sit, wait, and pray that Bigman would come back for him before the hostiles found him.

CHAPTER 24

Game On

Secret was finishing up the call he received from Mrs. Gomez. He was relieved it was her and not the old man calling to tell him that his days were numbered. She wanted him to confirm Amilia's pregnancy for her, which he was able to do because he had seen all of the tests Amilia had taken. The mother was happy to hear the news but got serious with him again telling him he needed to make Amilia stop what she was doing and bring her home.

Secret knew from the things Amilia was saying in the background that she wasn't going home to her mother because she believed she would only take the child from her. So all he could do was promise that he would make sure she was safe and as far away from things as possible. With that promise their call ended, but Secret's other phone started playing Uriah's ringtone.

"Hey, what up?"

"They found us. All of them are here now. We going to war with them fools!" Uriah told him.

"What do you want me to do with the bitch and the kid?"

"Nothing! I'm on my way. This shit ends tonight!" Secret told him after hearing the gunfire in the background before he ended the call.

"Papi, what's wrong? What's happening now?" Amilia asked, watching his face go from a soft expression to a hard one, just like that.

"They found where we're holding the bitch and the kid and came for them. I'm going to finish this shit before your mother tells the old man what's going on with you up here, and, well, you know that just can't happen," he told her as he rushed to get dressed. "And before you ask, no! Stay here. I'm going to end this, and we're going home."

Amilia didn't say another word. Once Secret was dressed, he grabbed his gun, keys, and helmet and then rushed out of the door. He decided to take his motorcycle, knowing the powerful crotch rocket would get him there fastest.

Amilia quickly dressed and rushed out a few minutes behind him. She saw the bike speeding up the block and got in her car, storming off behind it. She wasn't trying to catch up to him, but she didn't want to miss any of the action either, so she fell back just a few minutes behind him.

~ ~ ~

Dream's attention was drawn to the rumble of a speeding motorcycle as the four of them emerged unharmed from the building.

"Dream, do you still got bullets?" Bigman asked, trying to catch his breath while placing Leslie down beside a big black dumpster.

"Yeah, I still got two whole clips. Do you need one?" she asked, kneeling next to Rahji after putting her down to catch her breath.

"No, I'm good. But I gotta go back in there for Teema. I need you to promise me y'all gonna stay here until I get back," he told her while walking back over to the door.

"What if—?"

"If I don't come right back, then go that way. Get the fuck away from here and call somebody to pick y'all up. Don't come back in here," he said before he smiled at Rahji and said, "I'll be back."

He then rushed back inside.

They could hear Bigman blasting his gun before the door closed behind him, and the dogs began barking like crazy.

"Mama, is he gonna kill the bad dogs? Can we go home so Uncle Paper can take auntie to the doctor? Where's Trigga? Is he looking for us?"

Rahji shot question after question, going into shock from being so overwhelmed by everything.

Dream hugged her and did her best to try to calm her down while trying to wake Leslie with her free hand. That's when she spotted a car pulling over and parking not far from where they were hidden. When Dream saw Amilia get out of it, her anger was instantly renewed.

"Listen, baby, I need you to stay here with Leslie. I'll be right back, promise."

She could see the doubt in her child's eyes.

"Didn't I come for you this time?" Dream asked, pulling her phone from her pocket and texting Misty to call her ASAP. She then sent a mass text before giving Rahji the phone. "Make sure you answer all the calls; and if they ask, tell 'em where you are the best you can, okay?"

"Okay, Mama. I love you!"

"I love you more."

Dream hugged and kissed her daughter, and then

went in search of the reason for everything that had happened to her family and friends.

Rahji settled down next to Leslie. She wished she was old enough to have a gun while she stared at the door for Bigman and Teema to come back out. She didn't have to wait long for him to return with Teema like he promised.

"Rah-Rah, where's your mother?" Bigman asked while reloading his last clip into his gun.

"She said she'll be back and that she was going to make sure nothing happens to us again," she answered.

"What is she talking about?" Teema asked.

"I don't know," he answered him. "Rahji, which way did she go?"

"That way." She pointed toward Amilia's car. "She gave me her phone and told me to answer it if anybody calls too." Rahji held up the phone so they could see it. "Can you go get her too?"

Bigman told Teema to stay with them and gave him his Glock with an extra clip, just in case.

"Hey, I'ma take that car and get us the fuck out of here before we bleed to death. I'll call when we're somewhere safe. Now go find her so all this shit won't be for nothing," Teema told him as he watched Bigman run off in search of Dream. "Stay right here. I'm gonna go get us a ride to the hospital someplace," he told Rahji before he limped off toward Amilia's car, hoping to find the keys in it.

Although he knew how to start the car if he didn't find the keys, he was lucky they were still in it.

CHAPTER 25

The Confrontation

Trigga, Sam, and Paper broke away to re-group in the hallway. When the trio was all safely there, Trigga sent Paper and Sam to look for Leslie and Rahji while he went in search of Dream. During the gunfight, he noticed she had vanished from his sight along with Teema, and this was the hallway where he last saw them.

As soon as they split up, Trigga pulled out his phone and saw Dream's text telling them she got her daughter and Leslie out of the building and that they were outside behind back. He was just about to call Paper to tell him to meet him out back, when an unknown man suddenly appeared in the corridor standing only a few feet in front of him.

When their eyes met, Secret instantly recognized Trigga from the many surveillance photos he had been given of him over the years.

"You must be that nigga Trigga," Secret said with a menacing grin.

"Who the fuck is you?"

There were only a few quick moments of silence before Secret tried to aim his gun to shoot. Trigga dropped his shoulder and charged him, knocking the gun and wind from Secret. He plowed into his target's body, sending them both crashing to the hard, polished granite floor. Secret found the power to push him off of him and sat up to take a breath. Trigga recovered fast and rushed in at him again, this time swinging a hard fist at his head. Secret blocked two of the haymakers and then kicked up with both feet, connecting with Trigga's chest and sending him flying backward and crashing into a door. Secret then scrambled to his feet while simultaneously picking up and firing the gun at Trigga.

Trigga saw him going for the gun and vaulted into an open apartment door. He slammed the door shut to shield him from the shots he knew would follow.

"Put down the gun, and let's slug it out," Trigga yelled as he looked around for another way out.

"Open the door so we can do this."

"Fuck you, bitch!" Trigga said as he ran through the kitchen to the rear exit of the apartment.

He ended up in the corridor around the corner

from Secret.

Trigga spotted his own gun and phone lying on the floor right where he dropped it. He heard Secret send a few more shots through the door before kicking it open to come after him. That gave Trigga the opening he needed. He ran and scooped up his things just as Uriah and a few more thugs entered the hallway from the far end. Trigga blindly shot behind him as he ran away outnumbered.

~ ~ ~

Outside, the area was quickly flooding with MPD's finest. Police squads poured in from almost every direction toward the deadly disturbance going on inside the building. Detectives Bells and Rios made it onto the scene and rushed through the entrance, following behind the SWAT team. Once inside, the officers were caught in the line of fire. They spread out as they joined in on the gunfight trying to bring an end to the chaos.

Dream saw the police and took off running in the opposite direction. When she rounded the corner, she saw Amilia.

"Bitch, stop!" she demanded while catching up to her. "You put your fuckin' hands on my baby and my family for the last time!"

"No! No, please don't shoot," Amilia pleaded while turning toward her. "It's not like that."

"It's not like what? Bitch, fuck you! I got them, so I know how it is! Fuck you!"

Dream took her first shot and hit Amilia in her arm. The force from the bullet sent Amilia crashing to the floor.

"No, please don't kill me! Please, I'm pregnant!" she told her, trying to find compassion in her.

"Pregnant? So what! Weren't you just about to kill my baby to hurt me?"

"No! It's not like that. I was coming to get her and take her away from here. Look at me. I don't got no gun or nothing," Amilia said, holding her arm trying to slow the bleeding. "It was never my intention to hurt Rahji. You gotta believe me."

Dream couldn't bring herself to pull the trigger on the crying unarmed woman. She lowered the gun to her side.

"Why? Tell me why all this? Don't you think your punk-ass husband did enough to me? You know I didn't want him. I fucking ran away from him. Remember that? So why, Amilia?"

"Dream, I don't know. I was mad at you and blamed you for my daughter's death," she answered honestly. "It wasn't my idea to do this. Our children are brother and sister, and I'm about to have another. Please let me go. I promise I'll never come at you again," Amilia told her as she got back on her feet.

"On my baby, Amilia! If I ever feel like something happened because of you, me and my man will find and kill all of you," Dream promised her.

"Okay, please?"

Dream believed her, but then Leslie's badly battered face popped into her head. All of a sudden, she rushed Amilia, punched her hard a few times, and then head-butted her before pistol whipping her unconscious.

"Dream! Dream, let's get the fuck outta here! The police are everywhere!" Paper yelled.

Paper and Sam had just rounded the corner when they saw her beating Amilia with her gun.

"Let's go now, girl! They're coming this way!" Sam shouted, snapping her out of her rage.

"Okay, I'm good. Let's go!" she said, kicking Amilia in the arm before she ran off.

The three of them fled the building, running right

into a mass of flashing lights. Police cars were in every direction that they looked. They were just about to turn around and run back inside to look for another way out, when Trigga drove right through the fence. The big SUV came to a hard stop between them and the police. He didn't have to tell them to get in. Once they were all inside, Trigga put the truck in reverse, stomped on the gas, and spun it around, facing the way he came. Paper and Sam traded shots with the police officers closest to them as they raced off into the night.

"Wait!"

"We already got them. Teema just called and told me they're all at his mama's crib," Trigga answered, already knowing why Dream was telling him to wait.

CHAPTER 26

The Aftermath

Dazed and a little confused, Amilia stumbled out of the building and right into Detective Rios.

"Hey, freeze! Stop right where you are and hold your hands so we can see them!" Detective Bells ordered while pointing her gun in Amilia's face.

Amilia collapsed giving in to the dizziness. Two officers ran over and secured her hands before getting permission from Bells to escort Amilia to one of the waiting ambulances.

"Oh shit, man. They got Amilia!" Secret said to Uriah.

"I didn't know you brought her with you."

"I didn't."

All they could do was watch her being placed in the ambulance surrounded by cops. They both climbed on Secret's motorcycle and sped away from the scene before the police noticed them.

"So, what are we gonna do about Bossy? We can't leave her in there," Uriah said once they were safely in the parking lot at Secret's place.

"I don't know yet. I'm thinking about it. All I know is that I gotta get her outta there before she calls her daddy to do it," Secret told him, punching in the unlock code to the door of his building.

"Can't you do what she did for you or something like that?"

"That's what I'm trying to figure out how to pull off. Amilia's not an illegal like me, so I gotta come up with something else." He dropped down onto the sofa once they were inside the apartment. "Damn, man! I told her ass to stay the fuck here. Why couldn't she just listen?"

"Bossy knows you don't want her to call her daddy, so she might try calling you first. Don't you think?"

"Me or you, 'cuz she knows I don't want them to have my personal number, and I don't know if she knows this other one."

"Really? You just told me that she's carrying your baby. I bet she knows every number you got," Uriah told him, sitting in a chair across from him and picking up the TV remote.

"I hope you're right. Hell! They can't have shit on her but maybe a gun charge. If that's it, I'll pay your girl to go bail her the fuck out and let you get back to this shit up here once it cools down some," Secret said as he got up from his seat. "Do you want a beer?" he asked while walking to the kitchen.

"Hell yeah, since we gonna be playing the waiting game and shit."

~ ~ ~

From the hospital, Amilia was taken to jail and placed in the same interview room Secret was held in just days before. Just like with him, the detectives had left her in the cold room alone for over an hour before they came in to talk with her. Now Detectives Bells and Rios were sitting in front of Amilia going through the motions of trying to extract information from her. They hoped she could help them put the pieces together about what went down and how she fit into it all.

"Why were you there again?" Rios asked her for the second time.

"I told you, I was only there because of some guy I met at Silks where I work part time," Amilia repeated her lies once again.

"Yeah, you said that. But what I don't understand is why he would take you with him to fight in a gang war if he just met you," Rios said, taking a sip of his coffee.

"I don't know what that was in there. He told me to stay in the car, and then he went inside. After a while, I got curious and had to use the bathroom, so I went in. That's when all hell broke out. I ran, and then some guy I didn't know grabbed me. I tried to fight him to let me go, and the next thing I know I was handcuffed in the back of an ambulance."

"So you're a prostitute that works part time at Silks?" Bells asked, trying to get a reaction out of her that she could build off of.

"No. I don't fuck for money. Men pay for my time in the club, and if I happen to find one that's cute enough for me to let him take me out, I do that. But I dance for my money!" Amilia snapped before she shut her eyes and dropped her head in her hands.

She wished they would just leave her alone. She then wondered which one of them she could just pay to let her go.

"Well, Ms. Gomez, everything you say checks out so far," Bells told her after looking over her notes from the interview with Bigman.

"I told you!" Amilia said, fighting not to smile

and show her bruised face again.

"Yeah, nobody knows who you are. The only thing is the car you told us about is nowhere to be found at the scene. And since you didn't see the guy you were there with in the photo lineup, I think it's safe to say that he took off and left you there."

"I told you I think I forgot the keys in it when I got out."

This was the first truth Amilia had told them. She honestly didn't know what happened to the car, but she thanked whoever took it.

"Well, you're free to go, but don't leave town. I might have a few more questions for you later," Bells told her.

"Is there anyone you can call to pick you up, or do you need me to have one of the squads drop you off at home?" Detective Rios asked while still trying to fish information out of her.

Bells placed a landline phone in front of Amilia before she and Rios left the room. They watched and listened in on Amilia's call on the monitor in the corridor outside the interview room. They overheard her telling who they believed to be her father that she was okay and needed a ride from the police station.

"Papi, please hurry. I don't wanna be here anymore," Amilia told Secret, ending the call and hoping the detectives bought her act of talking to her father.

She knew they were listening in on her call somehow.

CHAPTER 27

A Follow-Up

Leslie was taken to the hospital and treated for all of her bumps and bruises. She had to file a police report about the story she fed the doctors about fighting off an attempted rapist that took her purse.

Dream was back to her old self now that she had her daughter home. Trigga asked her to marry him. She said yes and accepted his mother's ring that he inherited after her death. Trigga knew his mother would approve of the woman's hand he put it on. Rules was awake but still in the hospital. One of the bullets came very close to his spine and did a lot of nerve damage.

"So what you're telling me is I damn near had to die to get you to spend the night with me and to show me your love?" Rules asked Dana, who hadn't left his bedside for more than two hours for the week and a half that he had been in the hospital.

"Would you stop it! You know I had to play hard to get to see how badly you wanted me!" she told him, pushing his just-delivered lunch tray in front of him. "If I made it easy for you, would you still want me?"

"Hell yeah, I'd still want you. Have you seen that ass you got!" Rules's laughter brought on a coughing fit that hurt his lungs. "Look! Now you trying to kill me!"

"Shut up! Nobody's trying to kill you. You're alright. Now stop trying to get between my legs, and eat before it gets cold," she told him with a smile, shaking her head and crossing her legs.

"Oh, a nigga wasn't just trying to get between them sexy-ass thighs. You'll know when I'm trying. Hey, I'm not even sure if my dick is working right. Why don't you come give it a kiss and see if it wakes up for you?"

"Rules, stop it. What's gotten into you today? I'ma have the nurse come check your meds to see if your ass is high right now," she joked while smiling at him.

Before he could answer, the door opened after a quick knock. The nurse walked in holding a clipboard, and they both started laughing.

"What did I miss?" she asked, setting down her clipboard on the table beside his bed.

"Nothing! I just told his ass that I was gonna call you, and you showed up. That's all."

"Why—! You know what, never mind. I know him by now. How's he doing anyway?"

"Crazy and about to get punched!" Dana told her jokingly.

"Am I wrong if every day that I'm able to wake up and see her is a good day for me?"

"Can you please tell me your pain? You know how this goes, from 0-10," the nurse asked while adjusting his IV fluids.

"It's like a 3 right now, nurse. But wait!"

He looked at Dana and held out his hand to her.

"What do you want?" Dana asked, leaning forward as she held it.

"Please, Dana, do me the honor of spending the rest of my days with you?"

"Rules, stop it!" she said as she pulled her hand away like his was hot. "Let her do her checkup!"

Dana sat back in her seat.

"Okay, nurse, now it's a 10! My pain's to the max because she just broke my heart."

"You shouldn't play with people like that. I thought you were really proposing to her."

"Who says I wasn't?" he said, staring at Dana and not smiling.

"Let me do my checks so I can go. I don't have time for your mess right now," the nurse told him. "I got more people to see, so let's get on with it. Try to lift your left leg." She held her gloved hand over his toes a few inches and said, "Kick my hand, please?"

Rules did as she asked, bringing his leg up nice and strong. This was the usual, so it was no surprise. The nurse moved her hand over to his right foot and told him to do the same. This was the side that she was concerned with most.

"I can't! It hurts!" he said angrily.

"Raul, you didn't even try; and before you try and say you did, this morning you moved it. The movement was slight, but you did. I didn't say anything to you at the time because I didn't want you to hurt yourself so early. But now I need you to kick my hand so I can get the doctor in here to do his job."

Dana saw the look in the nurse's eyes and could tell that she was telling the truth about what she thought she had seen.

"Rules, baby, stop getting mad and try harder for me, please?"

"What do I get if I do it?" he asked Dana, unable to stay upset around her.

"I'll give you all the hugs and kisses you've been asking for. Nurse, you heard that, right?"

"You're my witness. I get all the hugs and kisses I want just for trying."

"Okay, yes! I heard her, but you have to do it or the deal is off! Right, Dana?"

"Right!"

Rules stared at his foot for a long moment in silence. The only thing that could be heard in the room was the steady beeping coming from the nurse's station just outside the door.

"Why you holding your hand so high. What the hell ever happened to baby steps?" he complained.

The nurse lowered her hand just a little, and Dana took out her phone so she could record it when it happened. She wanted to show him whatever little movement the nurse had seen to give him hope.

"Come on now! I'm not lowering my hand any more."

"Alright, here goes nothing."

He took a deep breath then gave it everything he had in him to kick the nurse's hand.

"Oh my God! Oh, Rules, you did it! He did it!" Dana sang out excitedly while shedding tears of joy.

"I knew I wasn't seeing things this morning," the happy nurse said, now patting him on the leg. "Now I need you to try to move it one more time. Dana, get ready because I need you to send me that video to show the doctor."

She put her hand back over his foot but higher this time.

"I know it hurts, but think about the kisses you're gonna get," the nurse reminded him with a smile.

His foot went up quicker this time and moved her hand. He let his foot fall, and he did it again and again until it just hurt too bad to try anymore.

"I can move it! I'ma be walking up outta this bitch!"

"Okay, okay! Let's calm down. You need to rest it now. I mean it, Raul! Don't try and push yourself any more. Rest! I'm going to talk to the doctor and show him the video so he can place you at the front of his busy schedule and come look you over."

The nurse grabbed her clipboard and then rushed out of the room.

"Do you wanna see it on video?" Dana asked,

already replaying it for herself.

"Hell yeah! Let me see my work!"

"I'ma send it to everybody, okay?" she asked excitedly.

"Yeah, they need to be ready for when I carry you down that aisle."

"It's walk me down the aisle, crazy!" she corrected him, before sending the video to everyone in her phone's contacts.

"I'm for real, Dana! I'm serious!" he said as he took hold of her hand again. "What I feel for you is real. I moved my leg because of you—because I wanted to make you happy. We don't gotta do it today, but please say yes? Knowing that I'll have you at the finish line is all the motivation I need."

"Oh my God! Yes. Okay, yes!" she agreed and then kissed him.

"Now that's your kiss. Can I get mine?"

"Yeah! I got you baby!" she cooed as she climbed on the bed with him, kissing him more passionately. At the same time, she slipped her hand inside his gown and stroked his semi-hard length until it stood tall and firm. "Now we know it still works."

"Baby, you can't leave me like this!" he told her after she stopped the hand job.

She grinned, tossed back the covers, and put her warm mouth to work. Dana didn't have to work hard or long before he was filling her mouth with his release. Between the pleasure of Dana's head game and the powerful meds kicking in, Rules passed out. He started snoring, so Dana relaxed. She thought there was something wrong with him and was about to call the nurse to help, but now she just let him rest. Dana watched the video over and over, and then imagined being carried down the aisle in Rules's arms.

CHAPTER 28

The Conclusion

Amilia was back in her Miami home with her feet up, allowing Secret to nurse her and pamper her back to her old self. Amilia's face was still discolored from the beating she received from Dream, but other than that, she was okay.

"I don't like this. I can't stand looking over my shoulder for your father to come for me like he did Cheez behind the same damn thing I let you talk me into."

"Papi, you told me you would do anything for me, remember?"

"Yeah, Amilia, how can I forget after what we just went through? I'm reminded every fucking time I look at your face," he answered, letting her feet fall onto his lap. "I still got you. As soon as it cools down up there, I'ma have Uriah end that shit for good for you," Secret promised before he then started rubbing her feet again with coconut oil.

"It's not that I don't want you to handle it, but just let them be for now. When I was sitting in that police room all alone, I thought about how Dream could've killed me or my baby, and what she said to me about just wanting to get away from Cheez. That woman just wants to live her life. I know now that she's not the reason for my pain. He was. He's the reason my daughter is gone. He's the reason I don't have my son here with me now. He's the reason all this isn't yours. He did so much to keep me away from you."

"Amilia, you lost me. Who are you talking about, Cheez, or that punk Trigga? I'm trying to follow you, but you need to put a name on it so I know who to focus on."

"I'm talking about that old washed-up man. Papi, it's time for this family to have a new head, don't you think?"

"You know I do. But do you really know what you're saying? Do you know how hard it is to get to the old man over there?" Secret asked her as he stood up and pushed her feet to the floor. "I know I could do a better job, but getting to him to take him out back home ain't happening."

"I don't wanna be talking like this, and you don't need to be getting yourself all worked up."

Amilia watched Secret walk over and stare at the exotic marine life inside the two-hundred-gallon aquarium. She was trying to come up with the best way to tell him that she had already set things in motion for him to deal with her father.

"I called and told him about Milwaukee last night," she blurted.

"You did what! Why would you do that, Amilia?" he asked in disbelief.

He quickly pulled out his phone and texted Uriah to come back to the house from his sightseeing.

"I did it so you can show me that you have what it takes to lead this family and to be my king," Amilia replied as she stood quickly, closed the space between them, and then pushed his phone hand down. She kissed him hoping he didn't push her away. "Do you love me?" she asked when he didn't push her.

"What?" he asked, not knowing if she had lost her mind doing what she had done without telling him.

"If you love me and this baby, you gotta fight for us. Choose us and make sure he doesn't make it back when he comes for you."

"You know I choose you. If it wasn't about you or this baby, I would still fight. I'm not lying down for no man. So tell me you really want this and make me believe it!"

She said nothing. She only kissed him with a hunger that told him all he needed to know. He scooped her off of her feet and carried her back over to the sofa while still locked in their kiss. When he laid her down, he pulled open her robe, knowing it was the only thing she was wearing. He then started kissing her belly and then slowly making his way downward.

"Yes, papi! Take what is yours! I want you to take it all!" she panted before pushing him from between her legs and turning around and getting on her hands and knees, face down and ass up.

Secret rubbed the tip of his length teasingly over her clit.

"Take what's mine. That's what you told me to do, right? Tell me you want this!" he called out as he continued playing with her clit with the tip of his hardness. He sometimes pressed it onto her opening, just to let her know how close it was to her getting what she wanted.

"Do it! Do it! Yes! I want you to take it!"

He pounded into her wetness from behind nice and hard, causing her to scream out his name in pleasure. Secret reached around her waist using his fingers to stroke her clit until he felt her warmth tighten and squeeze him before she came hard.

~ ~ ~

The doorbell rang two hours later. Shortly afterward, the maid escorted Secret's old friend Raymond into the family room where Amilia and Secret were sitting.

"So, he sent you here to do what exactly, Ray?" Secret asked, daring him.

"I'm only here to pick you up. Mr. Gomez is outside and would like for you to come and have a talk with him. Don't act like you don't know how this works. How many times have we done this?" Raymond told him, grinning like he had been waiting for this moment for a long time.

"Whatever, Ray! So he's not even going to come in and say nothing to me?"

"Amilia, he's not in the best mood right now. With this and the shit going on out west, it's just not a good time."

"I'm his fucking daughter! Just fuck it."

She put her hand on Secret's shoulder and then kissed him on the cheek before getting up and leaving the room.

"Amilia, can you make reservations at that place you like—the later the better? And try to get us a table facing the water," Secret yelled behind her before he walked out of the house with Raymond following close behind.

Outside, Secret spotted a silver Porsche Cayenne with dark tinted windows parked just off the grounds, and he smiled to himself. He then climbed in back of Mr. Gomez's black Lincoln Town ar. That's when he saw that not only had Raymond jumped ship on him but so did his man, Browny, who was driving the car with an unknown younger Mexican man sitting beside him in the front seat. Mr. Unknown was doing his best to look the part of a tough guy. Secret chuckled to himself.

"How you doing? You really didn't have to come all the way here to talk to me, sir. I was going to come see you as soon as Amilia was feeling better," Secret told the angry old man sitting across from him.

"I thought you were smarter than this. I told you

what I expected from you, Secret."

Browny pulled away from the house as the old man spoke.

"I can't believe I have to have the same conversation with you that I had with Cheez about my daughter," Mr. Gomez told him as he leaned forward. "I hope you said your goodbyes to her before you walked out."

"No, actually, I'm going to ask Amilia to marry me tonight over dinner. I wish you could be around to witness it, but she understands that sometimes you have to face death to really enjoy life. Amilia knows that I'll kill to live, so she'll be okay."

"I know. I taught her well," the old man said before he nodded to Raymond and the flakey thug quickly slipped a cord over Secret's head. "Fuck you!" Mr. Gomez said as the cord tightened.

"What the fuck! Agghhh!" Secret yelled as he fought and clawed at the cord around his throat.

"Shut the fuck up! You're sounding like a bitch right now," the unknown thug said, resting his gun over the seat while watching Raymond tussle with Secret.

"You did this to yourself. How could you be so

foolish? Did I not give you all I promised?" Mr. Gomez said, sitting grinning as if he was watching a live play.

Suddenly the Town Car was rammed from behind. The force of the impact made Raymond loosen his hold, giving Secret a breather and the distraction he needed to put in the work to save himself. Secret regained his composure, kicked the gun out of the young punk's hand, and then kicked him in the face, bloodying his mouth. Next, he threw his head back and slammed it into Raymond's jaw and chin as he struggled to get free of the cord. The car was rammed again, but this time harder, which caused Browny to lose control and spin out, hitting a few parked cars before crashing into a large palm tree.

Uriah slammed the SUV into gear and then jumped out, spraying the driver and passenger sitting in the front seat of the Town Car with bullets. He then snatched open the rear door just as Secret broke free of the chokehold. Uriah shot Raymond in the side of the head, killing him instantly to end the fight.

"I knew I wasn't wrong about you, Secret," Mr. Gomez said to him, trying his best to look unafraid like he was still in control of his life. "I guess I'll be witnessing that proposal tonight after all."

"Thanks for your blessing, but you were never gonna make it," Secret told him, picking the gun up off the floor. "What did you ask me when I got in the car?" He pretended to think about it. "Oh yeah. Did you say your goodbyes? Old man, you really should've gone in and talked to your daughter," Secret told him before shooting him twice in the chest. "It's time for a new king!"

He shot him once more before getting out of the wreckage.

"We need to make it look better than this," Uriah said.

"You're right. Let's make a statement. Light this bitch up!"

With that said, the two of them emptied their clips into the car, making the scene look more like a hit than a rescue. Then they got back into the Porsche and fled the area. Secret sat back in the seat, looking out the window at all he had just inherited as Uriah drove him back home to Amilia—his queen.

To order books, please fill out the order form below:
To order films please go to www.good2gofilms.com

Name: _____

Address:_____

City: _____ State: _____ Zip Code: _____

Phone:_____

Email:_____

Method of Payment: Check   VISA   MASTERCARD

Credit Card#:_____

Name as it appears on card: _____

Signature: _____

Item Name	Price	Qty	Amount
48 Hours to Die – Silk White	$14.99		
A Hustler's Dream - Ernest Morris	$14.99		
A Hustler's Dream 2 - Ernest Morris	$14.99		
A Thug's Devotion – J. L. Rose and J. M. McMillon	$14.99		
Black Reign – Ernest Morris	$14.99		
Bloody Mayhem Down South – Trayvon Jackson	$14.99		
Bloody Mayhem Down South 2 – Trayvon Jackson	$14.99		
Business Is Business – Silk White	$14.99		
Business Is Business 2 – Silk White	$14.99		
Business Is Business 3 – Silk White	$14.99		
Childhood Sweethearts – Jacob Spears	$14.99		
Childhood Sweethearts 2 – Jacob Spears	$14.99		
Childhood Sweethearts 3 - Jacob Spears	$14.99		
Childhood Sweethearts 4 - Jacob Spears	$14.99		
Connected To The Plug – Dwan Marquis Williams	$14.99		
Connected To The Plug 2 – Dwan Marquis Williams	$14.99		
Connected To The Plug 3 – Dwan Williams	$14.99		
Deadly Reunion – Ernest Morris	$14.99		
Dream's Life – Assa Raymond Baker	$14.99		
Flipping Numbers – Ernest Morris	$14.99		
Flipping Numbers 2 – Ernest Morris	$14.99		
He Loves Me, He Loves You Not - Mychea	$14.99		
He Loves Me, He Loves You Not 2 - Mychea	$14.99		
He Loves Me, He Loves You Not 3 - Mychea	$14.99		
He Loves Me, He Loves You Not 4 – Mychea	$14.99		

He Loves Me, He Loves You Not 5 – Mychea	$14.99		
Lord of My Land – Jay Morrison	$14.99		
Lost and Turned Out – Ernest Morris	$14.99		
Married To Da Streets – Silk White	$14.99		
M.E.R.C. - Make Every Rep Count Health and Fitness	$14.99		
Money Make Me Cum – Ernest Morris	$14.99		
My Besties – Asia Hill	$14.99		
My Besties 2 – Asia Hill	$14.99		
My Besties 3 – Asia Hill	$14.99		
My Besties 4 – Asia Hill	$14.99		
My Boyfriend's Wife - Mychea	$14.99		
My Boyfriend's Wife 2 – Mychea	$14.99		
My Brothers Envy – J. L. Rose	$14.99		
My Brothers Envy 2 – J. L. Rose	$14.99		
Naughty Housewives – Ernest Morris	$14.99		
Naughty Housewives 2 – Ernest Morris	$14.99		
Naughty Housewives 3 – Ernest Morris	$14.99		
Naughty Housewives 4 – Ernest Morris	$14.99		
Never Be The Same – Silk White	$14.99		
Shades of Revenge – Assa Raymond Baker	$14.99		
Slumped – Jason Brent	$14.99		
Someone's Gonna Get It – Mychea	$14.99		
Stranded – Silk White	$14.99		
Supreme & Justice – Ernest Morris	$14.99		
Supreme & Justice 2 – Ernest Morris	$14.99		
Supreme & Justice 3 – Ernest Morris	$14.99		
Tears of a Hustler - Silk White	$14.99		
Tears of a Hustler 2 - Silk White	$14.99		
Tears of a Hustler 3 - Silk White	$14.99		
Tears of a Hustler 4- Silk White	$14.99		
Tears of a Hustler 5 – Silk White	$14.99		
Tears of a Hustler 6 – Silk White	$14.99		

The Panty Ripper - Reality Way	$14.99		
The Panty Ripper 3 – Reality Way	$14.99		
The Solution – Jay Morrison	$14.99		
The Teflon Queen – Silk White	$14.99		
The Teflon Queen 2 – Silk White	$14.99		
The Teflon Queen 3 – Silk White	$14.99		
The Teflon Queen 4 – Silk White	$14.99		
The Teflon Queen 5 – Silk White	$14.99		
The Teflon Queen 6 - Silk White	$14.99		
The Vacation – Silk White	$14.99		
Tied To A Boss - J.L. Rose	$14.99		
Tied To A Boss 2 - J.L. Rose	$14.99		
Tied To A Boss 3 - J.L. Rose	$14.99		
Tied To A Boss 4 - J.L. Rose	$14.99		
Tied To A Boss 5 - J.L. Rose	$14.99		
Time Is Money - Silk White	$14.99		
Tomorrow's Not Promised – Robert Torres	$14.99		
Tomorrow's Not Promised 2 – Robert Torres	$14.99		
Two Mask One Heart – Jacob Spears and Trayvon Jackson	$14.99		
Two Mask One Heart 2 – Jacob Spears and Trayvon Jackson	$14.99		
Two Mask One Heart 3 – Jacob Spears and Trayvon Jackson	$14.99		
Wrong Place Wrong Time – Silk White	$14.99		
Young Goonz – Reality Way	$14.99		
Subtotal:			
Tax:			
Shipping (Free) U.S. Media Mail:			
Total:			

Make Checks Payable To:
Good2Go Publishing
7311 W Glass Lane,
Laveen, AZ 85339